CASSANDRA CIELO

FROM GOLDEN SKIES

THE CAT, THE PRINCE
BOOK 1

*To my mom from reading this long before it was anything close
to decent.*

*To my husband who supported me in writing this story for the
last 7 years.*

*To the friends that cared about these characters as much as I
along the way.*

Content Warning : There are depictions of violence and death. Heavy topics such as grief and loss. Though it is a closed door romance with no explicit scenes, there are some makeout scenes but characters do not go further than kissing on page.

MT. ARYTHMA
WYCLIFF
CITADEL
ORO
BEZER PLAINS
MT. ERAN
ERASMUS
MT. KIDRISOL
BLUE VOLCANO
N
E
W
S

COINANIA
TYNDALE
PALACE MOREH
KINGDOM OF SHAMAR
CASTLE JUDAHALL
ROMATH
KINGDOM OF GOLAN

PREFACE

"Haybale. Hayyyyybaaale."

I moaned and rolled over, desperate to get away from the nagging voice. Unfortunately, I had fallen asleep on the chaise, and not my usual spot on the lounge, so instead of rolling into plush cushions, I tumbled to the hardwood floor with a *thunk*.

My brother laughed, towering over me, his shaggy brown curls falling into his hazel eyes as he continued to chortle at my expense.

Tiredly, I rubbed my elbow and shifted to sit up, when something snapped under my hip as I moved.

The last dregs of sleep vanished as I pulled the book I had fallen asleep reading from under my side. It flopped pathetically in my hand, cracked along the spine, the pages crumpled and bent. Oh no. The poor book. I would have to pay damages to the library for it.

I frowned at the sight of my ruined book and sent my most withering stare at my brother. It wasn't that the book had great value, it was just the history of trade routes between the cities of Shamar. Still, it would be difficult to finish now with the pages nearly falling out.

"Theo, stop pestering your sister and go help your father in the fields!" Mom called from the kitchen, knowing, even without looking, that Theo had done something to annoy me.

My brother straightened his broad shoulders and held his hand out to me. "Just a minute, Mom!" he yelled back as he yanked me off the floor. I smacked my nose into his stupid oversized shoulder. He used to be so dang, scrawny, gangly and weighed down by sicknesses, but that all changed in the last few months, now at nearly eighteen he was massive, and at times my mind couldn't rationalize the change.

"Happy seventeenth birthday, Haybale." He grinned, pulling a wrapped bundle from behind his back that I hadn't noticed. The golden wrapping glistened—he must have spent a pretty penny on it.

I took it, a mix of dread and excitement warring inside me at receiving the present.

Today wasn't just my birthday.

"Open it after I leave," Theo warned, and pointed his finger accusingly at me, as if I had already snuck a peek somehow.

I took in the slim military-grade Krav uniform he wore and the looming sunrise out our old farmhouse windows.

They would be coming just after breakfast.

"Why give it to me now if I can't open it?" I whined, trying to hide my disappointment and dread. We'd known this day was coming ever since Theo got the vibration gift, a power that manifested at the age of fifteen, but knowing that didn't make his leaving any easier.

The front door opened, and my dad, hulking and more broad-shouldered than his son, walked down the hall. The thud of his work boots made the worn wood floors creak in protest. He rounded the corner, and I took in the same green-hued Krav uniform on him that was on Theo.

My dad's salt-and-pepper hair was braided tightly down his back, a style I had started copying for my own golden blonde hair, at the age of seven. A style I had maintained since.

My father smiled brightly at me, cupping my cheek as he walked by. "Morning, Haya." He kissed the top of my head. "Happy birthday, baby."

"Daaad..." I hated when he called me "baby," just as much as when Theo called me Haybale, a nickname he and our friend Micah had come up with when we were ten and I fell off the barn loft into a pile of hay. Unfortunately only my small ego was bruised, so the name had stuck. I liked to think if I had actually hurt myself, the event would not have turned into a joke and my subsequent nickname.

"I was just about to come out." Theo sighed as our dad turned to him.

"Theo, there is so much to get done," Dad chastised.

"We will be fine, Dad," I assured him. "Mom and I can handle the farm."

"Of course you can, you will have to, but I'm going to do as much as I can before we go. We won't get leave until the fall, and that is going to be too late in the season for most of the harvest."

"I got it, Dad," Theo said, and begrudgingly left the living room. Unlike with our father, the floors barely creaked under his feet, as if he was using his gift to make his steps as silent as a winter night.

We listened to the front door close.

"Sleeping on the lounge again?" Dad smiled.

"The chaise this time." I frowned, holding out my book to him.

"You will need a proper night's sleep going forward. You and your mom will have this whole farm to manage."

"We *will* be okay," I assured him again.

"Haya, breakfast is almost ready, did you finish your chore—" Mom called, her voice getting closer as she moved from the kitchen into the living room. Her light hair was clipped up, and the dusting of summer freckles had only just started their yearly appearance over her nose and cheeks.

She rubbed her hands on her apron as she took in my father's uniform, her words faltering. Bright green eyes, eyes I had inherited, glistened with tears I knew she had already shed the night before. The sound of her sobs on the front porch still rang in my ears, but now she swallowed them back and cleared her throat.

My father had re-enlisted at her request, even though it was the last thing she wanted. She'd asked because of Theo. Because all his life he had been the sick one, the weak one, the one she had to worry and fret over. Now he was strong enough to go to war, and just like me, she could not rationalize the fast change in him. She'd asked my father to re-enlist with him, to keep him safe. I understood well enough now that it hurt her more than I could understand to have been the one to ask my father to enlist again.

"Haya?" Her voice cracked a little as she glanced at me.

"Not yet, Mom," I said, answering her question about my chores. With a forced smile, I quickly placed the present and book I was still holding on the chaise.

"My girls," Dad said with fondness, opening his arms to bring us into his embrace.

I winced. The love in those simple words were like a

knife to the chest. I could see the same pain mirrored in my mom's face. The pain of saying goodbye when it was not yet time to, but the end was near and inevitable.

He wrapped an arm around both of us and took a few deep breaths.

"Sadness could blanket the whole day if we let it," my father whispered. "But today is a wonderful day—today my second favorite golden-haired girl was born." He beamed, smiling down at me.

There were so many families who had lost a parent already to the war. I had been lucky enough to have both my parents, to see their love, for the last seventeen years. To be cared for and protected. I was so grateful to have had them both, especially when every day I saw the effects of war. The children orphaned, spouses widowed by the endless fighting between our kingdom, Shamar, and the southern kingdom of Golan.

The war might last forever, but at least the mandatory service to the kingdom was only two years long. Our family would be whole again if they could make it through those two years; my father had done it once before. He could do it again.

I pressed my face into his chest, desperate to remember this moment, to hold on to his memory.

Two years, we just had to make it work for two years, then they would be home, they would be back with us again.

"Your father's right, sadness cannot win this day." Mother rested her hand on my shoulder. "Haya." I braced myself for words of wisdom or words of love. "What is that in your hair?"

I turned out of the embrace and shifted my long braid over my shoulder. A pencil stabbed my arm before slipping from the twisted locks and dropping to the floor. Pieces of straw and scraps of paper like confetti were shoved carelessly into the long plait.

"Theo..." I rolled my eyes to the ceiling, exhaling in frustration.

My mom stifled a laugh.

"Mom," I whined.

"You're always such a good sport." Dad chuckled. I glared but laughed a little myself. Theo had been shoving random things in my hair since I was a kid. This was nothing new, in fact it was oddly comforting.

Mom plucked a few sticks of straw from my hair. "Clean up and come for breakfast, you can do your chores after." She smiled, her eyes curving into half moons. It was a real smile, and though Theo was the most annoying older brother ever, I was grateful he'd given us this moment, a moment of normalcy, a moment of genuine happiness on my birthday.

I hurried up the stairs with my present. Once in my room, a simple space with a desk, wardrobe and a bed, I placed the package on the windowsill, looking out at the farm below.

Our farm, The Golden Farm, sat at the edge of town and abutted a vast forest that traversed the white-capped mountain range, Amaranth. In a few months the wheat stalks would turn our little stretch of the valley into a sea of gold that would sway in the wind, giving homage to our surname.

For now it was shaping up to be a warm summer day with a cloudless sky of blue and growing fields of green.

I made quick work of the mess in my hair, dropping the scraps of paper onto the sill next to my gift. I cupped my hands to gather the strips of paper and toss them away, when the dirt road leading to our farm clouded. An open coach led by two black stallions was barreling down the path.

They were not supposed to come till after breakfast. The sun had barely risen.

Panic seized my chest as I turned from the window to run down the stairs.

I stood on the porch as the coach came to a stop.

Theo and my father stood at attention in the grassy yard.

I felt my mother's presence as she joined me on the porch, but my attention was on the copper-skinned woman holding the reins.

The open coach was empty save for her.

She jumped down, her landing no louder than a leaf falling to the dirt. It was clear she was very skilled with the gift, her movement fluid and deadly. She wore adornments of metal across her arms and legs, a symbol of status in the military.

"Sirs, I apologize for the early arrival, however, you are to leave on the first train to the capital today. I thank you for a swift departure." Her short red hair was slicked back, curving just behind her ears.

"Understood," my father answered, clasping her arm just below the elbow in greeting. She did the same in return, a standard hello in Shamar.

I shook my head, confused. This wasn't how it was supposed to happen. We were supposed to have the morning. We were supposed to have more time.

"Armond?" My mom stepped forward, meeting my father on the steps of the porch. She held a wrapped box that smelled of the breakfast she had made inside. My shoulders sagged in defeat. She was always prepared for everything, ready to support and take care of whatever was needed.

"Love." My father smiled while taking the box. "Thank you." He kissed her forehead.

"Haya, come say goodbye," she invited over her shoulder, her tone controlled, unfazed by the change in plans.

I ran to my father, wrapping my arms tightly around him. He had only a second to move the box of food out of the way of my embrace.

"Ha, okay, it's okay." His arms came around me, warm, safe. "You are as strong as anyone with the gift," my father whispered in my ear. A sweet encouragement he had been saying to me long before I hit the age of fifteen, the age when the gift manifests for those lucky enough to get it. I was not, but my father never seemed to mind that.

"Come home," I ordered, fighting tears and losing. Before I completely lost my nerve and started sobbing, I ran to Theo, wrapping my arms around him too.

He scoffed a little. "Haybale, you're so emotional, work on that while I'm gone, okay? If you leave Mom to do all the work on the farm by herself because you're too busy crying in your room, I will find out and kick your scrawny butt."

"That better be a promise, 'cause when you come back, we both know I'll kick your oversized butt twice over." My threat had no bite.

I felt him shake his head and laugh.

"Tell Micah bye for me. You two try not to get married while I'm gone," he teased.

I scrunched my nose.

"He'd have to get permission first," I teased back.

"Who says he hasn't gotten it already?" He leaned away so I could see his wiggling eyebrows.

My eyes widened, tears drying as my mouth hung open. He was joking, right?

"Trying to trap a bug?" he taunted, poking my cheek.

My mouth snapped shut. Was he serious? For a moment I was completely distracted, but that was probably the point.

I felt a gentle tug on the end of my braid; my father's way of saying it was time.

Shaking off my brother's ploy at a diversion, I smiled bravely at them and kissed their cheeks. With one final smile, they climbed into the coach.

My father leaned over the edge, giving my mom one last kiss. It wasn't a peck but a real kiss, one full of love. There was definitely tongue. Where it had grossed me out as a kid, I now was glad to see their affection, even if it was still a little bit uncomfortable. To see how much they loved each other, that it didn't matter who was watching, was something rare in this war-torn world. I could only hope for a love like theirs someday.

The rays of summer sun broke over the white-capped mountains as the horses led the coach away.

We were supposed to have more time, but now only time would tell if we would be rejoicing at their return or mourning it.

CHAPTER 1

Another Goodbye

The months that followed were a blur of hard labor and even harder moments of sorrow. Moments in which Mother and I took turns being each other's solace. We had received little to no communication since the first month of their service, and the season of harvest was quickly upon us. Even with the orphaned or children of widows helping through the summer months, we were woefully behind schedule. For years my parents had let many children come and help on the farm till they were of age for an apprenticeship, manifested the gift or found another form of work. Though they were children, my parents would give them work and pay them a wage to either be used to supplement at home or to store away for secondary schooling. Mother and Father could have hired actual laborers, but they always tried to be fair with the work on the farm, as there was more to be done than our family alone could handle. It was our farm that supplied all the wheat from Wycliff to Tyndale, a city to the east shore.

Father would say, "It's only right to help out the sons and daughters of my fellow soldiers. We have to take care of each other in times of war." Those in the town took comfort from this, knowing that should the need arise for them to go and fight, we were here to help care for and support their children.

It also made for an interesting upbringing, as many of my first friends, first crushes, were children hired to assist on our farm. It was added work, managing a "staff," especially one as unruly as children, but the joy they brought to our little valley was always greater than the challenges. Besides, my mother managed the schedule of responsibilities while I got to play with the children and manage the ledgers in my father's stead. It was expected that one day I would be taking over the farm.

Two swift thuds against the front door roused me from where I slept on the lounge. The stupor of sleep lifted sharply as the ledger I had been working on the night before tumbled off my lap and onto the worn wood floor with a smack, the pages bowing. I rubbed my eyes in the dim blue light of morning—normally my favorite time of day if not for the persistent banging on the front door. I sat up, a twinge in my neck from sleeping the night in a skewed position.

Who would be here this early? I rolled my head side to side.

I could faintly hear my mom rustling in her room upstairs.

Swinging my legs over the fallen book, I straightened, dusting off my work pants, which I had been disinclined to remove yesterday, knowing I would only have to don them again. My long honey hair tossed about my face as I attempted to sort myself out for the visitor. With deft haste, I smoothed the twists of the long plait that hung to my hips and moved down the hall to the door.

A knock, more firm than the last, startled me as I reached for the knob. The knock seemed to reverberate through the door and down my spine, making my skin prick, hot and tingly, with alarm.

An armored man peered down at me from the threshold; past him, his horse's bated breath rose in white puffs in the chill of the early morning. The cold ground clung to the dew as mist wafted from the fields. The steed's powerful legs kicked the ground, mud coated up to its knees in a spotted pattern of brown and red. I took in the man before me, my eyes fixating on his boots, which were caked with the same dried red mud. Mud not native to the north of Shamar. Red mud was only found at the border of Shamar and Golan.

Mud found at the front lines.

A deep sense of dread welled inside me.

I shifted nervously under the man's gaze. "Sir." My voice cracked. "Can I help you?" I asked, brow furrowed.

The creaked steps of my mom coming down the stairs quelled my rising unease.

"Is Mrs. Jean Golden home?" The soldier's baritone rang out, commanding attention. His dusty pale eyes were rimmed with dark bruises, his pallor hidden under dirt and sweat. Why had he ridden by horseback? Our town had a perfectly decent train. The metal of his armor and chain mail, a testament to his high rank, clicked together as he squared his shoulders.

Before I could speak, my mom was at my heels, gently

but with a firm hold pulling me from the doorway. She gestured for the soldier to come in.

"Obliged," he said, and removed his pauldron and breastplate as was customary when entering a home. Mother took them and quickly passed them back to me, my arms shaking under their weight.

"Put those down, dear," she said softly to me, not meeting my eyes. She kept her head turned to the man and after a moment answered his question from before. "I am Mrs. Golden. What news have you brought me?" Her tone was all business, her short hair clipped back, accenting her high cheekbones and pale skin freckled and sunburnt from days working the fields. The labor we both had taken on more diligently with my father and brother gone. Even my skin, which rarely burned, held a pink hue from the summer sun.

The soldier angled himself in the narrow hall between my mother and I as if to block me from what he would say next.

I turned, shuffling back to the lounge to place the armor down. The metal plates clattered together, muffling whatever the soldier said next.

My eyes fixated on the gold crest embossed on the pauldron. The king's crest. Unconsciously my fingers traced the deep gold cuts in the metal: the symbol of a large cat with two sets of feathery wings. One set covered the beast's face while the other set covered its back and sides. Something about the crest had always unnerved me. Beautiful as it was, always portrayed in brilliant gold, it was a symbol every child knew well because it was the symbol that took brothers and sisters, fathers and mothers away to fight. Still, it was uncommon to see the crest etched into armor. Most soldiers wore durable slim-fitting materials able to withstand vibrational attacks.

The material was commonly made in a shade of black or earth tones most conducive for camouflage. That had been what Theo and Father wore when they left. Metal armor was for decorated soldiers, more for show than for fighting.

Shaking my head to clear it, I lifted my fingers from the etched crest, and hurried down the hall.

Mother held a note, the wax seal of the City of Erasmus hanging ominously—black and shiny, from the letter's edge— as she scanned its contents.

My chest squeezed in trepidation, and I turned into the kitchen, needing to busy my hands, unable to just stand there waiting for her to finish reading. Shakily I poured the soldier a glass of water. We were nothing if not hospitable, and it was clear the man was weary.

When I returned, Mom had tucked the letter into the pocket of her work pants.

"You will be my escort?" she asked, and I searched her face for a clue as to what the letter said, but Mother was good at keeping her emotions in check, a trait I worked hard to model.

The soldier nodded in agreement. "We will leave at once," he announced, glancing at me. I looked up at him and attempted to smile as I held out the glass to him, the water trembling in my hand.

He nodded his appreciation and tipped the drink back heartily.

Unable to take it anymore, I turned to Mother, eyes wide. "Mom—" I began.

"Haya, could you ready my horse?" she said smoothly, taking off her apron and handing it to me. She pulled her heaviest coat off the wall rack, though it was not yet cold enough for such a garment. Winter was still many weeks away. It was only in the last few days that fall had begun to make its temporary home in our valley, changing the leaves from lustrous green to vivid red, yellow, and orange.

I bit my lip. "Is it Father? Theo? Are they okay?" I asked, helping her with the buttons of the coat.

The floorboards protested as I followed Mother into the kitchen. She hurried through the motions of gathering food and water for her journey. From the amount of provisions, I wondered how long she planned to be gone.

"Yes. They have been hurt," she answered gently, but her swiftness told me that hurt was a severe understatement. "I am going to the hospital in Erasmus."

The hospital just north of the front lines? What had taken them there? They were supposed to be at the capital. They were supposed to be out of harm's way.

"I don't know when I'll be back," she added.

"I'm coming with you," I said, grabbing more dried meat from the pantry and shoving it into her satchel.

Something flashed in her eyes, as she looked at me. "Haya," she said, a heaviness to her tone that made my hands pause over the latch of the bag. "While I am gone, don't leave the farm. If you need anything from town, ask Micah to get it for you. I will stop by to see his mother at the Citadel and let her know to look in on you while I'm gone."

"I'm coming with you," I said again, ignoring her.

She put her hands on my shoulders, stopping me in my search for more food. "I need you here," was all she said, and my resolve crumbled. I would not fight with her. I was small and soft like my mother, but she had a fierceness in her that I was too young to have fully developed. I was headstrong, but she had a doggedness that rivaled any soldier, or better yet salesman. I had never won a fight with her, and though everything in me screamed to go with her, I knew I would not start winning against her now.

So I nodded obediently.

"I will stop at the Citadel on the way out of town and have Mrs. Ilsan check in on you," she said again, and smiled, her green eyes crinkling at the corners.

"I'll be fine on my own, you don't need to ask Mrs. Ilsan to come," I assured her, trying to lighten my voice, trying to be as controlled as she was.

She searched my eyes before pulling me into a tight hug, her pale hair tickling my nose.

"Promise me you will be safe," she whispered, and for a moment she seemed more concerned for me than for Father or Theo.

My palms started to sweat. I wanted to ask her what the letter said in detail. I wanted to understand the lengths of their injuries, to demand I go with her, but she had made up her mind and there was no changing it.

"I'm counting on you to take care of yourself and the farm," she added, and squeezed me tighter.

My heart hammered, disquieted by her fervor.

"When have I ever not?" I sighed. "Come home and bring Father and Theo with you," I whispered, knowing what I asked was not in her power to deliver.

Still, she nodded.

I pulled away, forcing a smile on my face though it was the last thing I wanted to do. She did not need me to fall apart, not when my father and brother needed her more. I would wait until she sent for me, because surely she would if their situation became serious enough.

"I'll get your horse ready." I turned to grab her supplies but my hair snagged.

My long golden braid caught the buttons of her coat sleeve. My mind flashed to the day Father and Theo left, to the pencil that had fallen to the floor, to the scraps of paper and the present still unopened, sitting untouched on my sill upstairs. I felt like somehow that day was repeating, except this time the war would take my mother away too.

Gently, with a slowness the situation couldn't afford, she freed my hair from the buttons. She was always doing that for me, pulling out the annoying or painful parts of life so I wouldn't have to. This time was no different. The braid fell back to my side, hitting my hip in a familiar way.

She patted my shoulder, saying nothing, and left the kitchen, returning to the waiting soldier.

For a heartbeat I stood there, holding my braid with both hands as if it were a lifeline to happier, easier memories. Memories from before my brother got the gift and ruined everything.

I watched after her. Would this be the last time I would see her? The same thought snaked into my mind as it had the day Father and Theo left. No. No. I would not think the worst. Not yet. I pulled on my braid, letting the tug at my roots clear my mind. I grabbed her bag and slipped out the side door off the kitchen to the stables.

"Supplies are very low at the front." The baritone of the soldier carried over the golden wheat, making me pause at the stable door. I could see my mom and the man on the porch but could not hear the question she asked. "Erasmus's base has been having issues getting supplies from Romath. Trains haven't been running for a few weeks now. We have had to make do," the soldier replied.

My brow furrowed. What was going on in the south?

"I'm sorry," he continued. "It will be a long journey on horseback."

As if hearing this, the black steed he rode padded up next to me, pushing its nose into the grass, eagerly eating its fill for the road ahead. I pressed into the barn, knowing my mom would not have approved of eavesdropping.

In the stable I filled a bucket of water and returned to the horse outside. The poor beast would have to face the long hard journey again, and I couldn't help but pity him the crossing through the mountains.

I set the water pail down at his hooves. His flint eyes mirrored his master's; tired, grieved, and I wondered if all soldiers appeared as this man and steed did. I tried but could not imagine my father's chortling face dispirited or Theo's soft hazel eyes hardened. But the reality of battle was not something my quiet life could comprehend.

"Drink," I coaxed. "Come on. I know you are thirsty," I whispered, freeing the black mammoth's mouth from the bit. He eyed me the way only an animal could when it was calculating. Seeming satisfied with me, he dropped his large inky head, drinking steadily. I ran my fingers through his cropped black mane, feeling the coarse hair thick with dirt. If I had more time, I would have washed and brushed him till he shone with a stallion's robust air.

So many things I would have done if I had the time, but time ran from me even as I readied my mom's horse. Time ran faster than the hooves that carried both the soldier and my mother down the dirt road, away from our farm. Time ran faster than the speed at which my mind registered all that had transpired. Time ran the warm sun up the axis of the sky, lifting the cool tones of the night from the fields. Time ran as

I twisted the ends of my hair between my fingers, wishing I could have gone with her.

Time. A thief and a gift.

It pressed down on me as I sat on the porch staring at the hoofprints in the dirt.

I sat numb, my eyes unfocused as I gazed down the road, the dust of their departure long dispersed.

Time had been a friend my whole life. Making the days long for work and play. Giving me memories and moments with the people I loved. So why did time feel so fractured, so elusive now?

Time was not on my side anymore.

No. Time had an edge.

An edge, sharp enough to cut, and I was only just beginning to understand how deeply as anxiety meandered through my bones, making me wonder if it would become a permanent resident in my body.

The war had finally caught up to time and had taken my father, brother, and now my mother from me, leaving me for the first time in my seventeen years completely alone.

CHAPTER 2
The Tip Of A Sword

The pounding of hooves on the dirt road drew the attention of my dazed mind.

When had the sun's hungry rays spread over the tall wheat, dawning a new day?

"Haybale!" Micah, a family friend since I was ten, called, waving his hand high over his head as he raced down the path to the house.

He pulled his horse, Etienne, to a stop in front of the porch.

My heartbeat stuttered in my chest as Micah dismounted, jolting me out of my dark haze. I drank him in. His light yellow shirt, stretched over muscle, contrasted his coppery ecru skin, constant despite having lived in the north for years. His flaxen hair bounced wildly around his head, tousled from riding. Though I had seen him all summer long, it was only now that he was the only family I had left that my thoughts towards him turned to the words Theo had whispered the day he left. Warmth spread over my cheeks at the memory.

Micah was only six months older than me but most of the time he acted like he was twice my age. And though we only spent the last seven years together, it was like we had been friends since infancy.

Our fathers had fought together in the war, and when Micah's father passed away only two years after coming to Wycliff, we made Micah an unofficial member of the Golden family. And just like that, he had always been with Theo and I. We were inseparable, with Micah spending as much time at our house as he did with his mother and sister in the town.

"Micah." I sighed, feeling like I had taken my first real breath all day.

"I came as soon as I heard. Are you—" He stopped himself, partly because I had rushed him, jumping up and throwing my arms round him in a desperate embrace, and partly because he knew I would say I was fine when we both knew I wasn't.

"I'm glad you came." I pressed my face into his solid form, needing the contact, breathing in his familiarity.

He exhaled and wrapped his arms tightly around me. We had embraced many times before, but in recent months these touches, these moments were different, intimate in an easy way they hadn't before. I'd had a crush on Micah for years, but he never seemed interested in returning my affection in the way I wanted. I was positive he only saw me as a sister, but what Theo had said had me questioning every look, every embrace anew. We each had dated, sort of. For my part it had only been one boy who worked for a summer on our farm when I was fourteen, but by then Micah had already woven his way into my heart. So much so that I refused to have my first kiss with anyone but Micah, much to the other boy's disappointment. Three years later with no progress to that end had me wishing I had just gone ahead and kissed the boy from all those years ago.

Micah stiffened, and I realized we had been entangled in each other's arms far longer than normal, even for us.

I cleared my throat, taking a step back. "I could use some help." I gestured to the farm, knowing Micah would've helped regardless of my asking.

"No problem," he said coolly, walking past me over to the chicken coop and filling a basket with eggs. I fidgeted with the end of my braid but followed after him.

Hands deep in the nests, he spoke. "My mom said she will bring over dinner for the week, so you won't have to worry about that."

"That's really sweet of her." I nodded, mentally ticking that off of my to-do list. Feeding myself had been another concern cluttering my mind. Not that I didn't like to cook, it just always took me forever, and I, without fail, always made a mess. "Whatever she brings, I will love."

"Of course, my mom's cooking is the best," he said, placing the last egg in the basket, and brushed his hands off on his dark pants.

"Second only to my mom," I teased.

He feigned a look of horror. "You would pit Mrs. Golden's cooking against my mother's? I cannot condone such blasphemous words."

I elbowed him, and we laughed. Micah was the surest medicine to make me laugh. It was easy to have a bright mood when I was around him. All the tension from our awkward— at least for my part—embrace was completely forgotten.

We made our way back to the house and began the full day of work on the farm. The day passed in that busy numb way that makes one wonder if they have lived at all.

Micah had been helping out on the farm for years, so it was nothing new for him to spend the whole day till sundown tending the fields with me. As the sun signaled its descent, Micah and I returned to the house to wash up.

"Oh, I almost forgot," Micah said, jogging over to where Etienne was grazing. He unlatched a large satchel, tossing it over his shoulder. I walked inside to the kitchen sink, listening as Micah followed and heaved the bag onto the kitchen table, shaking the vase of wildflowers. "Here are your books for school." He pulled a stack of books from the pack. "I think you will like this year's history book, it's a new one."

"School?" I asked, confused. School started later in Wycliff, as we were a farming community and the harvest season dictated everyone's schedules. That meant the final year of my schooling—or at least it would have been, had my family still been here—was set to start early next week.

The school was in town, and regardless of my promise not to leave the farm, I'd already known there was no chance of me attending this year even before Mom's sudden departure. With Theo and Father away, there was far too much work to be done. So it was decided I would miss school this year. Which wasn't all bad. It wasn't as if I planned to go away to an advanced learning program or trade school. I had a trade; farming. I didn't need to spend time and money to figure out what I wanted. Everything I was supposed to want was right here on this sweet stretch of valley. Land many generations of my family had tended to. So my education need only consist of how to run a farm, something school didn't really teach. If I was honest, I was not all that sad about being done with school. Besides, the only part of school I enjoyed was reading.

"I thought they wouldn't let me finish from home," I

explained, recalling the letter the school administration had sent my mother.

"Come on, Haybale, this town loves your family, of course they made an exception. Just get the assignments done. I'll bring them in for you. If you get stuck on anything, I'll help you."

Micah was brilliant, he seemed to know everything the teachers taught before they even taught it. Like he had already graduated four or five times over. "The teachers are willing to make it work so you can still graduate this year, so don't blow it." He ruffled my hair annoyingly.

I swatted his hand away playfully as he gave me an easy smile. I could hardly protest when he smiled like that, so I took the books, wondering when I would even have time to do homework.

"What were you saying about history class?" I asked, shuffling the books in my arms.

"The book changed this year. You know how there's so much mystery behind the king's death? Well, this book has some speculations about the royal family and how the war started thousands of years ago," he said conspiratorially.

My brow furrowed. It was commonly understood and taught that the history of Shamar was mostly conjecture. Some things were fact, like the gift—because it was tangible, real, still happening today—while other things were lost to time and legend, like how the Donisi War started two thousand years ago and how both the king and queen died.

"I'm surprised they put theories in a history book," Micah continued. "Nearly everyone associated with the royal family is dead or missing." He looked at me expectantly, as if I would have something to say about a bunch of dead guys alive over two hundred years ago.

"Why history got all muddled to begin with is the real mystery." I shrugged dismissively. "Do you think the king's Seraphs messed with time when they traveled to the other worlds?" The Seraphs were said to have been gifted by the Creator of Strings to travel across space and time. To other dimensions. It was fantastical, yet widely believed. It was they who had laid the foundation for all the advancements Shamar had enjoyed for the last thousand years. Long before I was alive, the Seraphs were killed in the Donisi War against our neighbor to the south, Golan. After the passing of King Roark two hundred years ago, our world fell into a one-hundred-fifty-year span of peace. A peace that ended fifty years ago when the armies of Golan rose up, slaughtering and burning seven villages south of Romath, our capital, putting us in a state of war once again with Golan.

"I think there's a lot of things we don't know..." he whispered, looking perplexed.

"We at least can take comfort knowing the steward would not have approved the change without reason," I said, struggling to hold all the books. When Micah made no indication of continuing the conversation, I added, "I'll just take these upstairs."

My steps were quick as I bounded up the stairs to my room. Once inside I walked the length of my small bedroom, the hardwood unsettled under my steps. The walls were a light cream, matching the naturally worn wood furniture. I deposited the books on my windowsill, my unopened present glittering in the orange glow of the sunset.

I looked out the window at the golden wheat ready for harvest swaying in the wind, the valley surrounded by majestic mountains making it hard to imagine that swords and killing, blood and death were happening anywhere in the world.

A rhythmic knock of one-two, one-two echoed behind me, like a heartbeat.

I turned to see Micah standing in the doorway, knuckles poised against the frame.

I smiled at the familiar game. When we were kids and Micah would sleep over, after Theo had gone to sleep, we would tap the adjoining wall in a rhythmic language known only to each other. The one-two, one-two was a greeting; a one-one-two-one-one meant Theo was snoring. We had a myriad of codes developed over the years, and though as we had gotten older the game became less frequent, as Micah slept over less and less, I was pleased to know he had not forgotten our pastime.

I tapped on the sill in an easy two-one-two-two pattern that meant something to the effect of "let's get some milk and cookies." It was my favorite code then and now.

Micah tilted his head and pulled a plate of shortbread cookies from behind his back.

We both laughed.

After a beat I began to walk to him, just as he moved to enter my room. The strangest thing happened then—we both hesitated. A tension, like a steel cord pulled taut, had us both unsure what to do.

Micah had been in my room many times before, but never without someone else home.

The expression on his face indicated he was having the very same thoughts as I.

"I can go back downstairs?" he offered.

This was ridiculous, Theo's words were seriously messing with my head. Micah did not see me that way.

"Don't be silly, come in." I nodded, waving him into my room, like I had many times before, but unlike all the times before, the moment his foot crossed the threshold my palms began to sweat. I glanced frantically around the room for a place to sit, but everywhere I looked seemed unsuitable for some reason or another. The bed was too presumptuous or inviting, but if I sat in the desk chair, that would force him to sit on my bed instead, which seemed just as bad.

Micah's knowing eyes took in my fluttering, and with a tight laugh he set the plate of cookies down on my nightstand.

"I think I should go."

Panic filled me as he turned to leave.

CHAPTER 3

All You Had To Do Was Stay

"N o, I—"

Micah paused and raised a single brow, his expression almost smug.

I sobered and rolled my eyes. This was Micah.

"I hate eating cookies alone." I crossed my arms and sat decidedly on the edge of the bed. My braid flopped over my shoulder, the end pooling in my lap.

Micah dropped into the chair at my desk. "Twist my arm." He grinned.

I passed him a cookie, and we ate in silence for a few moments.

"Micah," I hedged, not sure I wanted to know the answer to the question plaguing me since Theo had left. "Do you regret not going with them?"

It wasn't common, but those without the gift could enlist, though it was generally considered suicide.

Micah lifted his chestnut eyes to mine, a serious and steady look I didn't quite understand in their depths. "Theo wanted the vibration gift more than anyone I have ever known. He looked into many paths that could take him out Wycliff. He didn't want to be here. It was suffocating to him. He would have left regardless of getting the gift, and it wasn't my place to go with him or demand he stay." It was almost rehearsed, almost as if he said these things for my benefit.

I had grown strong living on the farm. Loving the farm, but Theo had perpetually poor health and felt trapped in our town. He wanted to see the world. Getting the gift had been his ticket to that freedom.

When Theo's vibration gift manifested, we were all excited for him. My father most of all. He seemed almost relieved that at least one of his children ended up getting the gift. But unlike the other kids, Theo's gift did not manifest in a traditional way. His gift presented itself well into his sixteenth year, and for a time it seemed to intensify his feeble state. It took over six months for his health to improve, but once it had, nothing could stop him from enlisting to train at the Citadel, which being only an hour away wasn't nearly far enough for him.

Father had always told us that the gift took time to understand and grow accustomed to, but once Theo's health improved, he excelled exponentially. It was as if he'd had it for many years instead of a few months. Mother and I were told Theo was so gifted that he was allowed special military priority. Father assured Mom and I that there was nothing to worry about, that it was an honor. We were told they would be stationed at Romath, nowhere near the front lines. But clearly something had changed.

"Do you ever wish you had gotten the gift?" I asked, looking down and stretching the holes of my knitted coverlet.

When Micah and I turned fifteen, we did not get the gift. A friend of my father had offered to take me, with his daughter, to a special school designed for one to learn vibrations, the manifestation of one's soul, the gift. It was lengthy, expensive and not a guarantee. I had tried not to take it personally when my father refused to send me away. I still remember the fight he had with his friend on the porch.

"You need to give her a fighting chance in this world!" his friend had yelled.

"She has one. She has me and Theo to take care of her. She doesn't have the gift, and I'm glad for it!" my father, normally calm and reasonable, had yelled back.

"You're only hurting her by not giving her the choice."

"She is fifteen. I've never agreed with preparing a child for war at such an age."

"If you keep her locked up here on this farm, she will never amount to anything."

"She amounts to everything that really matters. I'm proud of her and the lady she is becoming. I'm sorry you don't see your own daughter that way."

"You're being unreasonable," the other man had said, his face a horrible shade of red.

"No. My friend. No. I would not send her off to the battlefield to face those monsters. I would not subject her to that life by choice. I wish you well, and I hope one day you can look at your daughter and see the precious gift she already is." When the door slammed, I had run back up the stairs, my own face flushed from hurt and pride.

My father never once talked to me about the offer, and I never brought up that I had overheard it. At first I had been too angry to talk to him about it, but later when Theo had gotten the gift and I saw how his life turned upside down, I heard my father's words in a new light. He loved me and was proud of me just as I was. He wanted nothing more from me than for me to be his daughter, smiling and reading the days away. When Theo got the gift, he was bedridden for the first few months, barely able to sleep, suffering from nightmares and unable to eat. I had taken on more responsibility on the farm. It was during this time I gained a new appreciation for my role. My family needed me more at the farm than on some far-off battlefield. Still, I felt the lack of the gift every day. It was the one thing children looked forward to the most. Getting the gift, having power, fighting the bad guys. But I was okay with my books and the tedium of life on the farm.

Micah shifted, grabbing the glass and the water pitcher I'd left on my desk, his back to me. "I often wish I had gotten the gift," he said, pouring the water and chugging it down.

"Lately I wish it had been me and not Theo," I whispered. The anxiety of the day seemed to stretch inside me like the holes in the blanket I fiddled with.

I didn't really want it to be me. I wasn't a fighter, I was an acceptor. I was good at accepting things, things that were hard. I was complacent. It was my special gift, but lately my personal special power wasn't working. I couldn't accept the feelings of loss assaulting me. I was doing everything I could to stave off my doubt.

Doubt that they would ever come home.

Micah turned and leaned his forearms on his knees, the veins and muscles in his arms shifting with the motion. "I don't. I'm glad it wasn't you," he said fervently, and I glanced up to meet his eyes. "You are safe."

I sighed, frustrated by his words. Being safe meant nothing when the people you loved weren't.

"Theo is probably dead because of it. Because he had the gift. If I had it, I could have gone with him, protected him."

"If your father, with all his medals, couldn't protect him, what makes you think you could have?"

I flicked a loose string, aggravated by the truth in his words. My father had gotten four golden wings upon his discharge. He was a skilled fighter even though his father and grandfather had only been lowly farmers their whole lives.

"I can do nothing for him. Either of them."

"Theo made his choice. He didn't have to go when he did. He was not required to serve for another year. He could have trained for a full two years if he wanted, but he didn't. He chose to enlist before he turned eighteen. He wanted to go, he thought he was behind because he didn't start training at fifteen like everyone else. But he didn't have to go when he did. That was his choice. Your father didn't have to re-enlist either." Micah moved to sit next to me, my bed shifting to accommodate his weight. Gently he laid his hand over mine.

"I just wish I could do more." I frowned, looking down at our hands.

Using his other hand, he lifted my chin, forcing my eyes to meet his heavy gaze. "You have no idea how much you are helping them now by just being here. Taking care of this huge farm mostly on your own. I'm proud of you."

I nodded, and though his words didn't comfort me, they did buoy my self-regard.

He looked like he wanted to say more on the topic but stopped himself, instead turning to slap his palms over his knees with a harring *smack*. "What poor timing." He sighed. "You need the extra help around here." He gestured, indicating the expanse of the farm and not just the house. "I could ask the kids to come back this week," he offered.

I blinked, surprised by the sudden shift in mood.

"No, my parents always give the kids off the week before

school. I don't want to be the one to break that tradition." Wycliff only had one school, where all the kids attended grouped by age. In the summer the kids would spend all day at the farm, but during the school year they would only come for the afternoons. This arrangement was so well known and appreciated by the community that the school would send their only bus to the farm just to drop the kids off.

I took comfort knowing that next week at least five of the seven days our home would be full of life and light once more instead of the eerie, empty thing it was quickly becoming.

"I want to honor how they would have done things. Besides, the kids need a break, this summer was not just hard on me and Mom."

Micah nodded.

"Well, I'm going to leave Etienne here with you. I hate keeping him in town anyway, doesn't seem fair to have him locked up when he can roam free here." Micah stood and smiled, walking to the door.

"Micah," I started to protest, unsure if it was his leaving Etienne or his leaving in general that I was against.

"I hate that you're here alone."

You could stay, I almost said aloud. Instead I nodded gratefully, eased slightly by the idea of having Etienne around. The horse was the last gift Micah's father had given to him before he passed. Ever since, rider and steed were inseparable. So it said quite a lot that he would leave Etienne with me.

I walked Micah out of the house and to the gate, waving as he left. The road back into town was long, but he knew the way well.

Once he was gone, I trekked on shaky legs to the top of the dandelion hill—at least that was what Theo and I had dubbed it. The hill sat a bit higher than the valley and rolled right up to the dark dense woods that traversed halfway up the white-capped mountains of Amaranth.

I looked out over the field, musing on the best strategy to tackle the abundant harvest. Freeing my hair from the tight braid, I sat among the flowering dandelions, it was unusual for them to be seeding so late in summer. My mind drifted away from the harvest below to the dusty road Micah had walked away on. How I wished to not be alone with my thoughts. With the sinking feeling of uncertainty and loneliness. Gnawing emptiness chewed at my insides like a living thing feeding off my sorrow.

I sat and waited. I waited as the sun splashed the sky with vibrant pinks and purples. I waited despite the cold wind. I waited even as my stomach growled for dinner. I waited long after the stars had graced the sky with their presence. I waited each night for the next week, finding my way up the dandelion hill at the close of another day. I waited despite knowing in my bones no one was coming back.

CHAPTER 4

Counted Sheep. Counted Breaths

My brother, Theo, and I sat on our hill. The one that overlooked the entire farm. Our favorite spot, covered in dandelions because it was the only place Father would let them grow wild. We lay in the grass looking up at the night sky. The stars were bright, dancing above us. But instead of being our eighteen and seventeen years of age, we were ten years younger, pointing, laughing and trying to name the constellations of the summer sky.

The dream was so normal, so real.

How many times had Theo and I done just this until our parents called us in for bed?

"I'm sorry I wanted to leave." I turned my head towards Theo, surprised. His curly dark hair shadowed his eyes. All he ever talked about was leaving the farm.

"Don't be. It was your dream."

"I'm sorry I didn't tell you about my secret." He sat up and looked down at me, his face still that of an eight-year-old.

"What secret?" I sat up too. It was funny to be talking so seriously in our child bodies.

"It's why Father re-enlisted."

I frowned, not understanding. "He enlisted to keep you safe."

"No. It was because I was gifted." Theo's voice broke on the word gifted.

"Gifted? Yes, you got the vibration gift," I agreed excitedly.

"I think this burden will fall to you now." He grabbed my hands and I watched as his face slowly changed. He was not a little kid anymore but the young man who'd left not so long ago. His face was resigned as behind him our farm went up in flames.

"Fire!" I cried, pointing at the flames. I could see a glow far off in the distance. Everything was burning. The fire moved so quickly. Everything in the valley was burning, not just our farm. The entire town was aflame. I scrambled to my feet. "Theo!" We were no longer children, and I reached to pull him up from the ground.

Theo lay back in the grass next to me, his face agonized. Was he hurt? I knelt beside him. His skin was damp with sweat, eyes unfocused. My hands fluttered over his body, not sure where to touch.

I wanted to embrace him. Lift him out of the chaos and carry him to safety. Tears poured down my cheeks, just as they had done the day he left the farm. For four months he had been gone. For four months, our house no longer felt like home. Within those four months the life I had lived for the last seventeen years had come to a quiet and unsuspecting end.

Theo's eyes squeezed shut, and though I did not hear him screaming, I could tell he was. I frantically looked around for help. Everything was pain and destruction. The rumble, sizzle *and cracking of nature burning drowned out all my senses. Flame's hunger unquenched until all was smoke and ash.*

I woke with a start. Sweat sprinkled my brow, my nightgown cold and damp against my skin. I pushed the covers off and walked over to the window, letting the chill of the early morning dry the tears on my cheeks. That dream... no, nightmare, had been too real. The warmth of the flames still licked at my skin, and I trembled. Each day was getting harder than the next to stay focused on the farm and my responsibilities. I wanted to run to Erasmus and bring my family back myself.

The nights that followed were riddled with more nightmares, the same destruction, the same fear, the same helplessness.

Our hill was covered in blood.

The trees seemed to come to life, moving as wraiths through one another until they were a solid mass of darkness. I stood barefoot on the wet grass, my nightgown stained red at the hem. My hair hung loose around my face as I stared into the darkness of the trees. The darkness looked to be breathing, rising and falling in the still night.

I was alone.

I was trembling.

I was frozen in terror, tears rolling down my cheeks.

I screamed as I woke, skin crawling as if eyes were everywhere around me, watching. I shot out of bed, running to my window, which was open, curtains swaying in the breeze, and I latched the lock. Shaking, I stared out at the tree line, a perfect replica from my dream. There had been something in those trees. I was sure of it, as sure as knowing my own name. Something had been hunting me. My heart pounded in my chest, and the pulse of blood sloshed in my ears.

I turned, jumping at my reflection in the mirror beside

my desk. My hair had come loose in my sleep and hung free about my face as it had in the dream. Slowly I twisted, checking my nightgown for the stains of red, but naturally there were none. It was just a nightmare.

Though I crawled back under the covers, I did not sleep the rest of the night. I sat awake, my knees pinned to my chest, trying to remember how to breathe. I counted sheep. I counted my breaths. But soon another day was starting, a nervous knot twisting violently in my chest.

When the sun finally rose, I got out of bed, my body dragging from the lack of sleep. I went through the motions of getting ready, braiding my long hair and dressing for another day of hard labor.

I barely ate. I moved through the day in a daze.

The morning passed quickly. Growing up on a farm, I was used to feeling busy, and tired. Work hard, rest harder was my father's motto. Although the resting hard part was rare.

I took no breaks, as I made up for my missing family members. After lunchtime, I heard the small school bus coming down the road. It was old, and very loud. Technology was much more advanced in the cities. Tales of sleek automobiles and underground roadways circulated the gossip mill, though I had never seen any. The kingdom did little for its people outside the major cities, however each town was given one bus per school as transport for the children. For this we were grateful, and it did seem to support the stories people tittered about.

First off the bus was Micah, as he had been leaving Etienne with me the last week.

"Good afternoon, Haybale!" Micah called, stepping off the bus. He wore faded work pants and a green shirt. His blond hair was smoothed back in a clean-cut kind of way. I tried not to laugh at the new hairstyle.

"Hi," I called, waving my free hand as I walked back down the path from the chicken coop, basket heavy in my arms. A few hens who had not been producing the last few weeks had finally started, and thus there were more than I could carry in my normal morning trip.

He jogged down the path to me, shaking his hair loose from the coif style. When he reached me, he took the teeming basket.

"Another beautiful day in Wycliff, don't you think?" He announced happily. Micah was without a doubt the most good-natured person I had ever met, and I smiled at his cheerful demeanor.

"Did something good happen to you today?" I nudged his arm and followed him inside to the kitchen.

"Well, don't be mad," he hedged. "Mr. Golden asked me to handle some things for him while he was away. One of which is the distribution of goods."

My brows shot up. That was a huge responsibility. My responsibility.

"You are still the numbers gal, don't worry. Think of me as the delivery boy," he placated, seeing my look of surprise.

"Dad asked you to be the front man, didn't he?" I clarified, pointing to his now uncoiffed hairstyle. He had been meeting with buyers.

He absently touched the back of his head. "You're mad."

I considered that. Honestly I didn't think I was. I had more than enough to do, and if Micah wanted the job of being the family liaison, then I wouldn't turn down the help.

"No, no, I'm not. It's for the best. I'll manage the ledger, and you handle the deliveries. Strings knows we have a lot of stock piled, ready to ship out." I gestured vaguely in the direction of the barn.

"Well then, no time like the present." He patted my shoulder, turning to leave, but stopped, twisting around.

His chestnut eyes scrutinized me. Could he see the oddly loose fit of my apron, the dark circles under my eyes? His gaze shifted to the empty sink, and I knew he'd determined something was wrong because I was notorious for leaving behind used dishes.

He opened his mouth, but just then I noticed the group of kids who had followed us quietly into the house, respectfully waiting for our conversation to stop.

My mom normally greeted the children and assigned their tasks, so I had completely forgotten that responsibility fell to me.

Micah glanced at me as if asking if I was okay. I gave a quick nod and turned to the children, squaring my shoulders, determined not to show how bone weary I was.

"Haya!" Olivia smiled and jumped into my arms, giggling. I positioned her on my hip smiling.

Olivia was only five. Her laugh was infectious despite the hardship her few years had already endured. Her mother had died in childbirth while her father was off fighting; he'd died shortly after Olivia's second birthday.

"Hey there, kiddo! How was school?"

"We learned all about Geo-gray-fee." She tittered as Micah patted her mussed red curls.

"You mean Geography," he corrected.

"Yeah." She gave a hearty nod, her chin bouncing off her collarbones. "There are three big cities in Shamar. Romath, Erasmus, and Tyndale." She ticked each city off her short fingers. "Tyndale is…" She glanced around the room, looking for a clear direction.

"East!" Tanna, one of our oldest at twelve, offered helpfully. Her mother worked as a seamstress at the Citadel while her father was stationed in the south. He had been out of contact for about six months; they did not expect him to return home.

Olivia nodded quickly in agreement. "East," she exclaimed as if she had recalled it herself. "They don't have mountains like we do. They have plains, they grow cows!"

I snickered.

"They don't *grow* cows," Erifin, a boy of eight, protested.

Olivia continued unperturbed. "Erasmus is south of us and is a *big* city with big desert rocks around."

"Desert rocks?" I mused, knowing she meant canyons.

"Mhm," she pressed on, "and Romath is the capital city. It's pretty, the teacher said all the buildings sparkle like rainbows. They put shiny rocks in the walls."

The other kids chirped in, filling in pieces Olivia had missed, like how the cities all focused on a different trade and industry. Erasmus: metals and clay. Tyndale: fish and cattle. Romath: wood and precious stones. Deep in the woods surrounding Romath were caverns filled with rare stones. It was what they used to make the city glitter in the sun. Though I had never seen Romath or Erasmus, I had read enough books detailing their unique beauty and trade specializations. It was necessary research for me to take over the farm.

Hickory, a quiet boy of ten, shifted on his feet. "From the late king's castle in the middle of the city, the teacher said you can see all the way to Golan." He peered up at me as if asking if it were true. I had no idea, as I had only ever been to

Tyndale, but I supposed it was possible, with the border being to the south and the tower being quite tall from what I'd read.

Micah interjected on my behalf, "You bet it is." His family was from Romath, as was my mother's kin. I hoped one day to see the spectacular city for myself.

"Now let's get to our chores today. Miss Haya has a lot on her plate so we shouldn't keep her." He gave a quick kiss to the top of Olivia's head, silencing the small girl, who was still chattering. Then he did the same to me, and for an instant we both froze. Time seemed to still as we both realized what he had done. It was no doubt simply habit from the many times he kissed the top of his sister's and mother's head in one motion, but I was most definitely not one of those two, and by the way pink spread over his cheeks, he realized that.

Sparing us both the embarrassment, I hastily put Olivia down and turned to the kids, giving Micah the chance to collect himself.

"Okay, who wants to help me thresh some wheat?"

After divvying up the things on my list and giving all the kids a snack, we got to work. Micah had slipped out the side door and took the plow out to harvest. We both would pretend the kiss had not happened.

After threshing for hours, I returned to the kitchen. Fall was in full swing, and to keep with tradition I whipped up some cinnamon orange bread to give to the kids, as my mom did every year about this time. The whole house smelled of sweet spices as I baked. I took the time they were in the oven to clean the bathrooms, dust and tidy the whole house, even venturing into Theo's room to give it the once-over. I wanted to make sure everything was ready for Theo and Dad when they came home.

The screen door opened and closed. Micah walked in, kicking dirt off his boots before coming inside.

"No, no. Shoes off, I just mopped the floor," I called to him, sounding like my mother. I waited for the thud of his boots on the porch before greeting him at the threshold. "Here." I padded over and shoved a piece of the bread in his mouth.

"Mmm." His eyes went wide. "This is really good," he mumbled as he chewed.

"Don't sound so surprised." I laughed while walking with him to the kitchen.

"You made all these?" He eyed the wrapped loaves of bread.

"Yes, and you can take home three." I held up my fingers to verify the number. "Please give one to your mom as a thank you for dinner last week."

I'd seen Micah only briefly in the last few days as his mom, Mrs. Ilsan, had come instead to check on me, leaving Micah home to care for his younger sister, Misha. Micah's mom worked two jobs and had enough to do, least of all be worrying about me. So after much assurance I would be fine, she'd stopped coming. The few times when Micah had come, there was more work than there was time to chat, so we barely saw one another.

Micahs' eyes narrowed slightly, scrutinizing me. Sensing he was going to say something about the brittleness he saw in me earlier, I popped a piece of bread in my mouth, and though I knew it tasted good, it was like soot in my mouth. I swallowed anyway, and he relaxed.

"Are you sure I can't take a few more? Looks like you made too many."

I pretended to count and then elbowed him. He would eat everything if I let him.

"Did you get a lot of the wheat packed?"

"Yeah, can you help me load it up? I'll take it to town in the wagon for you."

"That would be a huge help. If there is room, can you take the threshed wheat as well? I know it's not ideal, but I'm sure the bakers in town are desperate for it by now?"

"Of course, my lady." He gave a deep bow at my request. I laughed, wiping down the counter absently and gazing out the window over the sink.

The sun was still high overhead; the faint chortle of the kids' laughter met my ears, and for a moment everything didn't seem so forlorn anymore.

CHAPTER 5
Breath In. Breath Out

I dreamed the same terrible fiery dream every night in the weeks that followed.

Hope for a letter, for some news, clung to me like a leech, making me wonder if in the end it would be the hope that would kill me and not the physical strain my body was under.

Eating was nearly as impossible as sleep, and the toll it was taking on my appearance was more than a little apparent. Dark circles had made a permanent imprint under my eyes. Their luminous green was dulled and bloodshot.

Each day the house grew quieter, restless, heavy. Whether from the nightmares or my own loneliness, I was not sure.

Still, at dusk each day, I went up to the dandelion hill and waited till the sunset, willing their horses to come down the road to our home. The regret of not going with them, after them, picked me apart like a bird of prey with its next meal. I tried to overlay the image of the burning farm from my nightmare on the peaceful one I gazed at each evening. It was incomprehensible to me, but the dream bothered me deeply. I did not understand how something so horrible could be rolling around in my subconscious. I had stopped seeing my brother after the first nightmare. In that first horrible dream I had ached to hug him, and the longing to do so continued to grip me even after I woke, even after a week. There was nothing quite like a hug from a brother or father. It was like being wrapped in a blanket; a soft but thick barrier between the world and yourself. As if any impact could be lessened, something I was in desperate need of as the days pressed on.

I could barely recall the last hug I received. Micah had been keeping his distance since the kiss incident, and though he didn't do it to hurt me, it still stung.

Some nights, in an attempt to shake off the haunting quiet of the house, I would turn on the radio. It had been a sufficient diversion until last night's report.

"Nearly six hundred soldiers were killed, injured or are still missing in action after the attack last month. The incident is being investigated as to what the cause of the earthquake was that cracked the ground open, taking the lives of many on both sides of the battlefield."

I immediately switched it off, a wave of nausea making me curl into a ball on the lounge.

Somehow the days continued to pass, as if pausing for me to catch my breath was forbidden by some great power.

I lay on the lounge, another restless night behind me.

Rising with deliberate slowness, I moved through my routine. The bright sun shone overhead, the temperature a bit warmer than the last few days as I plowed the fields all morning, knowing Micah would take the bundles to town that night.

The squeal of metal and crunch of gravel had me looking

up. The children had arrived. I was dead on my feet as I shuffled to greet them. When the bus stopped, the kids and Micah hopped off, looking in high spirits due to the nice weather. My own spirits lifted. Their smiling faces were the only thing in the world that could bolster my strength. As I drew closer, I found them playing tag.

"Come on, kids, Haya is waiting!" Micah called, trying to corral them. They wouldn't hear it and continued their game.

"Ehem." The kids jumped, looking over at me as I emerged from the wheat stalks. "What do we have here?" I chided, giving my best displeased expression. For a second the kids looked chagrined. "I think..." I crouched low, wiggling my fingers. "... some chickens got loose on the farm. I better catch them before they get away," I threatened, reaching to tickle Olivia. Her eyes went wide as she scrambled away. Everyone squealed with laughter as I chased them around the front yard.

The children's laughter was infectious, and I could not help the genuine smile that stretched my face. Micah watched me with relief in his eyes. Had he noticed my distress the last few weeks? Had he seen me withering away?

"I think the rooster is loose!" I yelled, pointing at Micah, who was standing to the side of the chaos.

"A rooster has never looked so good!" he quipped, crouching low to join in the fun. "This good-looking rooster better herd up all the baby chicks." But instead of lunging for one of the children, he wrapped his strong arm around my waist, making me stumble.

"I'm no baby!" Olivia cried out as she grabbed his legs, making him lose his balance. The other kids circled around, jumping on my back, and grabbed our arms and legs.

"Oh no! I have been overtaken by the chicklets!" I gasped

in feigned horror as I fell back onto the grass, the kids tickling and piling atop me and Micah. We tried to parry their tiny-fingered attacks, but we were no match. Eventually the kids grew tired and fell on the grass next to us. We all lay catching our breath. The blue sky bright and cloudless, the warm sun danced across my skin. Everything was normal again, peaceful... ordinary, what it used to be.

"Haya?" Tanna asked, looking over to me. I sat up, slightly worried I might have played too rough with one of them. "Are you... are you sad?" she asked, her question catching me off guard.

Pain squeezed my heart, and the peaceful ordinary moment retreated as quickly as it had come. I had to close my eyes before I could speak.

"Of course not!" I lied. "I have all of you here with me." The cheer in my voice was very forced. The other kids sat up, looking at me with genuine sympathy in their eyes. It was not new to them, the loss of family to this unending war.

"Don't lie," Micah whispered.

"I miss Theo, Mrs. and Mr. Golden too," Olivia said, tears in her eyes. "Theo used to give me piggyback rides when I got tired." I moved to my knees and pulled her into a hug, giving the comfort I so desperately needed.

"I know, I know you do, I'm sorry." The other kids followed my lead till we were all huddled up. Micah locked eyes with me, finding my hand in the bundle of kids.

"But we all still have each other, that is something, right?" he said, his eyes not leaving mine. Did I imagine the affectionate look in his eyes?

I bit my lip, fighting the waves of emotion that threatened to overtake me. I would not cry. Crying would be accepting that something was really wrong, and I just couldn't do that.

It would be like accepting they were already dead. And I just couldn't believe that.

"Hey." I cleared my throat. "I have an idea—why don't I make you all some dinner today?" I offered, pulling away to look at all of them. Six sets of eyes appraised me, their sadness only slightly alleviated.

"But it's not the end of the week." Olivia sniffled.

I patted her head. At each week's end we would feed the kids before sending them home, as most shops would close before the day's work was done.

"Let's pretend. It can be our secret?" I held a finger to my lips. The kids brightened; it was the best meal they got all week, as most of them were lucky to have dinner to begin with.

Cooking the meal was a good distraction for everyone.

When we sat down to eat, it was a noisy affair, as it usually was with a room full of children. When we finished, Olivia fell asleep on the chaise while the rest of the kids cleared the table and helped each other with their homework.

"Haya," Micah said quietly so the kids would not hear. "We need to talk."

I shifted my back to him as I rinsed another plate. When I said nothing, he continued.

"I know you haven't been eating. Did you think I wouldn't notice?" He leaned against the counter next to me.

"Don't be silly, of course I ate," I said flippantly as I moved to wash the last dish. I had eaten at dinner, maybe not as much as I would have in the past, but chewing felt like too much work.

Micah grabbed the dish from my hand, forcing me to look up at him.

"Stop lying." I jumped a little at his fervor but recovered quickly with a smile.

"Really, I'm okay, please don't worry about me. I'm supposed to take care of you, remember. You're my employee," I teased, taking the dish back from him.

"Family takes care of each other," Micah said, aggravated, not buying my blasé attitude.

His words stung. "You're right." I nodded, appeasing him. "When did you get so wise?" I elbowed him, still trying to lighten his dark mood.

He glowered at the dish in my hand. "You can count on other people."

I took a deep breath. He was not easily distracted when he wanted to make a point.

I sighed. "I know. I just don't want you to worry about me. It's been weeks, and I haven't heard anything from my mom yet."

Micah nodded. We both knew that no good news by now meant only bad news was going to come. I just didn't know how bad the news would be.

"No matter what happens, you are not alone." He shifted to stand behind me, wrapping his arms around my shoulders. "You have people who care and love you," he whispered into my hair, sending shivers down my spine. I leaned back into his arms, needing the contact, needing his support. I was not sure where Micah and I stood. Was he saying he loved me? I mean, I knew he did, but was this real affection or something else?

We heard the kids giggle from the living room where they were doing homework, and for a moment I was genuinely at ease again. Light. The blanket I had been missing the last weeks enveloped me once more, making me feel safe. I turned in his arms, returning the embrace.

He stiffened, and I pulled back, searching his eyes.

His distant gaze focused as he seemed to clear out whatever thoughts had been distracting him.

"I almost forgot," he said, as if the moment we had just shared was nothing. "Your dad asked me to check the post office for mail for you and your mom from time to time. I figured your mom might have forgotten to tell you."

My heart leapt. Had there been a letter after all? Had my mom finally sent for me?

He shifted, reaching into his back pocket. "You have a letter from your pen pal—Talie, right?" He pulled the envelope out and waved it in my face. "I didn't even know you still talked to each other. How long has it been since you started sending letters?" he teased, holding the letter just out of my reach.

I shoved away my disappointment and reached for the letter.

"I don't know, like six years."

He ducked to the side as my hand grazed the edge of the long peach envelope. Talie always had the prettiest stationary. He shuffled backwards into the dining table, his annoyingly fast reflexes making it impossible to grab the letter.

"Come on, give it!" I lunged, catching my toe on the rug and knocking into him. He flopped back into one of the chairs, grabbing the edge of the table to keep from falling backwards. My eyes were fixed on the letter he held over his head, so I didn't realize the compromising position we were in till it was too late.

"Haya," Micah breathed, and I froze. I had never heard

his voice so husky and pained before. The letter he was holding fluttered down to the floor behind his chair.

I frowned, watching the letter fall.

I glared down at Micah, who watched my face shift to confusion.

Tenderly Micah's hand fell to my waist, and the soft pressure made me realize the position we were in. My legs had found their way to either side of his hips, and my torso had stretched the length of his as I had reached for the letter. And worst of all, my rear was planted firmly on his warm, solid lap.

My heart thumped aggressively in my chest as I scrambled to get off him, eyes wide. I took a few quick breaths and shook off my mortification. It was Micah after all, he didn't like me like that. The half-hooded expression on his face would have been there regardless of who the girl was on his lap. It had nothing to do with me.

Theo's words from the day he left flitted through my mind. No, no, Theo had been messing with me, teasing me.

Plastering a goofy smile on my face, I turned around to help Micah up. He knew my smiles well enough to know the ones I faked, but he didn't call me out for the one I gave him now. Instead he flashed his own tight smile.

I grabbed the letter off the floor.

"You're good to take the kids back and deliver the wheat?" I nodded, not waiting for his answer. "Good night," I rushed, throwing myself from the room and up the stairs in a frenzy.

Only once in my room with the door closed did I groan in utter embarrassment, throwing myself onto my bed.

The only thing keeping me from replaying the whole

embarrassing affair was the letter burning a hole in my pocket from Talie.

I sat up and opened the peach envelope.

Dear Haybale,

It has been exactly three months since your last letter. Your birthday has passed, and I have yet to hear any news of your father and brother. They were supposed to be stationed in Romath, correct? I asked some of my father's connections in the medical field about your brother's condition earlier this year. They said it was very unlikely that getting the gift is what made his condition worsen. Even more unlikely is the miraculous recovery. It was probably just a coincidence.

Please send me a letter soon. Life in Romath is as hectic as ever, sometimes I wish I were in the country-side with you. If we could switch places, I would in a heartbeat. I have lived so long in this stuffy house full of relics, and I'm not just talking about the furniture.

I hear Golan's army is growing every day, and I'm sure—well, everyone is—that they are planning some-thing. I don't know what changed, but in the last few weeks things have really stirred up. I wish I knew more to tell you, but do not worry about your father and Theo; if they are stationed in Romath, they will be safe.

And yes, I heard back from Cal, finally. He is doing great by the way, though I haven't seen him for nearly two years. He sent me a letter, apparently he is somewhere in the north. I like to think he is somewhere near you, safe in the mountains. Far from Golan.

To answer your question, yes, I am of marrying age. I haven't talked much about my love life, mostly because there has never really been much of one to talk about, but I feel I should reciprocate your confidence and tell you I have a crush as well. Like yours, he is a childhood friend. Cal's best friend, actually. He writes to me more than my own brother. Can you believe that? He is sweet but unfortunately does whatever my brother says, which drives me crazy.

I wish they would both just come home, but you know men and their adventures. I have hopes for a proposal upon their return.

Please write soon, I am worried about you.

Love,
Talie

I shifted to my desk, pulling out a parchment to write my response. My fingers hovered over the paper. My pen bled a dot of ink on the page, but no words came to me. I wanted to write. I wanted to tell her everything about my mom leaving, about the letter that took her away, about the pressure of the farm and the loneliness. Somehow I knew she would understand the loneliness best. But the words were too hard to write. My mind was too frazzled from the event downstairs with Micah. I sighed. I would try in the morning when my mind was clearer.

I listened to the front door closing and the sound of the wagon pulling away from the house.

Micah and the kids had finally left.

I let out a heavy sigh and began my evening stroll up to the top of the dandelion hill.

CHAPTER 6

Silver Cat

Though the day had been abnormally hot, the temperature had grown chilly, warning me of winter's imminent approach, by the time I settled in on the top of the hill.

I needed to finish getting the crops harvested before next week's end. I was already stretching my luck, as harvest time was past due. There was too much to be done. Even with the help, we were behind on our orders, behind in the work, and no matter how many ways I ran the numbers, we would lose more than half the crop this year to the quickly approaching winter.

I was beginning to wonder if I could keep any of my promises.

I understood my place but could not shake the guilt that came from being the only one not fighting. Father and Theo were fighting, possibly for their lives, and Mom was fighting to bring them home. What was I fighting for? The farm? I had promised to take care of the farm in my family's absence. I had promised my mom to not leave the farm for any reason.

I had promised to stay safe until they all came home, but fear and loneliness had a way of making even the best intended promises go awry.

The tears I had fought earlier that day pressed behind my eyes and burned to be let out.

I lifted my hands to rub away the tears. My right hand trembled. No, not quite trembled. The edges of my hand blurred as if it were not quite solid. I flexed my fingers, moving my hand, trying to disperse the illusion. A few errant tears had escaped, moistening my cheeks. It was simply a trick of my blurred vision, from the tears. I lifted my head to look out over the farm and nearly screamed when two large animal eyes locked with mine.

I was about to jump up and shoo the beast away to protect our chickens, as we had issues in the past with foxes, and the creature before me looked to be a silver fox. Upon closer inspection, though he had a tail fluffed and two-toned like a fox's, his face was much more akin to a cat's.

His puffed tail lay curled around his abnormally large paws. He was a bit bigger than your average stray cat. Perhaps some kind of wild cat? Most definitely not someone's pet.

His coat was thick and full like a wolf's; dark at the root but tipped in a warm silver, like a metal shield in the setting sun. It was most unnatural. But most alarming were his eyes. They were a deep black flecked with gold that glimmered in the faint light of day.

Like most cats, his gaze was piercing, but unlike most, I could barely see his pupils, which were round, a deviation from the usual black slits most cats had.

It was almost human.

I glanced away, unnerved. I should be scaring the strange

beast away, but instead I stayed still, hoping he would lose interest and leave on his own.

My heart quickened after a beat when I peered back and he was still staring. A little perturbed, I assumed he might be hungry. We had lots of stray cats on the farm. Most took up residence in our barn. They were helpful, as mice enjoyed hiding amid the wheat.

I stood slowly, not wanting to startle him, when a strong breeze loosened the seeding dandelions from their safe anchor and up into the sky around us.

His silver fur rippled in the wind, and a mesmerizing prism of colors glistened in the moving strands. I gasped as the colors appeared and just as quickly vanished. I rubbed my eyes again, convinced I was seeing things for sure now.

The sky overhead warned of the inky black of night as the first few stars winked down at us.

I glanced over at the farmhouse, which was hollow and empty. I was tired, sore in places I didn't think I could still get sore in, but most of all I was heartbroken. For my family, for the farm, for myself. Everything was falling apart, and all my attempts to hold it all together were weak, meaningless.

I peeked back at the cat.

This beast had come to our farm, to me, and something in that humanlike gaze had me taking a tentative step forward. He was probably just hungry, as he seemed to have come from the direction of the snowcapped mountains, where most animals were prepping for winter.

"Are you hungry?" I asked, moving closer.

He remained perfectly still. Had it not been for his breathing, I would have thought he was a very realistic statue.

Might he be injured?

Deciding he didn't look sick or diseased, I completed my approach.

He stared unblinking as I knelt before him.

His deep rolling purr met my ears; it was loud, almost as enrapturing as I imagined his roar might be. The sound made my bones soft, my shoulders relax and my thumping heart steady. My cheeks lifted in a timid smile. This was the most unburdened I'd felt in weeks, though I could not understand it. Perhaps this beast had some kind of special vibration ability, though the gift was unheard of in animals.

"Come on," I coaxed. "It's okay, I'll feed you." Encouraged by his purring, I reached out to pick him up, though I was not sure I would be able to lift him.

His still frame came to life, and I gasped as the ripple of his silver fur created little prisms between the strands again. His ears went flat, and he crouched, his head low and shifting from side to side as if telling me no.

I dropped my hands. I did not know what to make of this. Had he just shaken his head no at me? If I wasn't so stunned, I would have laughed. "Umm..." I hesitated. "I guess you don't like to be picked up?" That was normal enough—most wild cats I knew didn't like being picked up.

Tentatively, almost as if pained, he inched closer to nudge my hand with his head. My fingers curled just behind his soft ears. The silver of his fur was mesmerizing, I had never seen anything like it.

His ears relaxed, though his tail was still flat and low behind him. My hand slackened as he leaned into my touch.

"You're so beautiful," I whispered. My fingers splayed, pressing deeply into his thick fur. My hand dragged of its own accord, stroking down his scruff over the sharp bones of his shoulders.

He flinched, ears flattening again.

I pulled my hand away as if slapped, afraid I had hurt him somehow.

"A-Are you injured?"

He looked up, eyes almost accusing.

I peered around his body, careful not to touch him again. I didn't see any wounds.

"Okay," I said thoughtfully, holding my hands up in surrender. "You can follow me as long as you don't attack our chickens."

His purring was still very loud, almost as if it were inside my head. I blinked hard, trying to clear the sound away. My cheeks were hot. Why was I embarrassed?

A little annoyed at the whole encounter, I walked to the house, not checking to see if he followed.

At the door he padded up next to me.

"Okay, then." I smiled and opened the door for us.

The cat walked, sniffing the air and the floorboards curiously.

I glanced down at his fur just as a bug bounced to the small area rug.

"Oh no, you have fleas." I grimaced accusingly at the poor creature. He couldn't really help that he had fleas, most animals did, but my mom would not stand for them in the house.

I turned to open the door and send him back outside, when he looked up at me, eyes knowing.

I pursed my lips.

"You can stay only after I bathe you." I should just send him to the barn with the rest of the cats, but he was not like the other cats, and it seemed wrong somehow to send him on his way still covered in fleas.

"Deal?"

He sat down, his head tilting ever so slightly to the left as if considering.

"Wait here, I'll get the water warm." I was pretty sure we also had flea medication in the cupboard. I hurried from the hall into the washroom. Finding the flee treatment I added it to the water, and once the basin was full, I returned to the hall to see the cat still sitting and waiting.

I realized I had offered food before and should probably grab some, especially if I was going to try and bathe the beast. Though he seemed rather docile, he might have a great aversion to water as most other cats do.

Filling a bowl with chunks of chicken meat, I returned to the hall once more to find the cat gone.

The splash of water had me pushing open the ajar washroom door. The large cat was already in the tub, seeming quite content in the warm water.

His ears perked up at my approach.

"You're such a good boy," I praised, pulling a table over to the lip of the basin and placing the bowl of chicken on top. "You can eat while I wash you, okay?"

He seemed fully distracted by the food and did not even notice when I began to scrub his fur.

I should have been too spent from the day's events to even have energy to care for another living thing besides myself, but kneeling there, working the medicine and suds into his fur, watching the small bugs and dirt fill the water, I felt restored. Like somehow in mending this animal's bedraggled state, I remedied my own, even if just temporarily.

Satisfied with my work, though I could not reach his underside or legs, and he would not give them, I turned to get a towel and dry him off. I heard the slosh of water as he leapt out of the basin. Water splashed my back and soaked the floor. I hurried to make quick work of the mess.

Kneeling, I wrapped a dry towel around his body. After it was secured, he promptly left the washroom.

"Where are you going?" I asked, standing and following after him.

He bounded up the stairs and into my room. Once inside, he folded his legs and sank to the floor, eyes falling closed.

"I guess you're tired?" I sat on my bed and looked out the window at the sky, the hundreds of little stars coming out as dusk finally relented to night. I yawned. "Me too," I mumbled.

His purring, which had not stopped once, was as soothing as a lullaby, and before I knew it my eyes were drifting closed. My head fell to my pillow.

The whole strange encounter had given me a reprieve from thoughts of my nightmares.

So to the beautiful cat, I said a silent prayer of thanks as my mind and body gave in to sleep.

CHAPTER 7
Chicken & Names

The hill was covered in blood again. The shadows breathing in the trees seemed to disperse this time, surrounding me. I stood again in my nightgown, my hair pulled back just as it had been when I fell asleep. The dream was clouded, hazy. The awareness that I was dreaming was at the forefront of my mind, though my eyes couldn't see clearly. I blinked rapidly, trying to be rid of the haze, but it didn't help.

I turned, the shadows closing in. I ran. Like my vision, my hearing was all wrong. I could not hear the thump of my feet hitting the dirt, or the rustle of the trees. The only sound I could hear clearly was my own breathing. The gasps. The quick panicked inhales and exhales.

I made it down the hill and to the edge of the wheat before something snagged my braid, yanking my head back. The smell of burning hair permeated my nose. I gasped to see my hair singed at the end, the tie having burned off and the twists rolling loose around my shoulders.

I watched in horror as the shadow from the trees seemed to

grow out of the ground. I couldn't understand what was happening. The dark mass made no move to touch me again, but I sensed its violent intent. The black mass wanted me dead.

Confused, I stumbled back into the wheat, falling to the ground. I screamed as the shadow moved to stand over me. "No, please!" I cried, covering my face with my arms.

Someone called my name. The dream shuddered around me.

"Haya," the voice called. "Haya, wake up."

The dream continued, the shadow lunging forward, its form circling my throat as I screamed. I gasped for air, but nothing filled my lungs. The shadow was choking me. I was so cold even as my throat burned.

I was dying.

"Haya!" the male voice called again, this time with more urgency.

I faded between sleep and consciousness, following the ardent voice back to where I lay in my bed. Safe.

I woke fully with a shudder, the air I so desperately longed for filling my lungs. I felt something at my feet, and as quickly as I breathed in the air, it left my lips in a scream. I ripped the blanket off my legs and yanked my feet towards me. The room was still, a pregnant silence settled around me.

"N-Nothing's there..." I breathed out with a quiver. My body shuddered, and my eyes frantically searched the room for anything suspicious.

There was nothing, but I was certain there *had* been something in the room with me.

I could not shake the feeling that something was still watching me.

Gingerly, afraid of my own movements, I reached for the

blanket, pulling it over my shoulders, and turned on the side lamp.

Two animal eyes blinked up at me from the foot of my bed.

I screamed again.

The cat from last night simply waited for my hysterics to pass, head tilted lazily to the side.

"By the Strings," I breathed, calming down, as the prickling sensation of anger, embarrassment and fear subsided.

I had forgotten all about the stray cat I'd welcomed into my home.

Silence filled the room like a lead weight after my outburst.

We both sat perfectly still for a while, the nightmare deceptively filling the quiet with whispers of pain and terror.

I shivered though my blanket cocooned me and the side light illuminated the shadows. I still was cold to the bone.

My eyes filled and blurred, but I did not blink; the tears fell from my eyes, carried down by their sheer weight. I breathed through the tears, suppressing the burning sobs in my throat. These tears were too heavy to hold in, but I would not break down. I would not let the horrible nightmare terrify me to the point of breaking.

The stray cat stood and took the two strides to where I sat curled against my headboard. Gently he pressed his head into my shoulder. He radiated warmth.

I crumpled, wrapping my arms around the beast, forgetting that it was a wild thing, that I should be more cautious, and sobbed into his fur. I curled my body around him till his warmth was touching me from head to toe, like an oversized stuffed animal I had as a child.

The sound of my sobs only made me sob harder, till after

some time, I rested my head against the wall, weary and empty.

I felt the rumble of the beast's purrs against my chest; his velvety ears brushed against my cheek, causing me to pull back. The large cat quickly moved back to the other side of the bed, seeming satisfied that my outburst had subsided.

I chewed my lip and glanced around my room once more. It was still dark out, but the air held the light crisp feel of early morning. The sun would rise in a few hours.

Convinced nothing in my room was going to harm me, I determined to do something useful with the time.

Deciding I wouldn't burden her with all the recent events—though if I had, I knew she would understand—I got up and penned my return letter to Talie. After writing a short nondescript response about recent weeks, I turned my attention to the homework I had let pile up. I worked till my dream was almost forgotten, and the sun peeked through the window. All the while, the beautiful cat lay stretched out across my bed, purring softly.

———

I spent the day in the fields with the kids. We had a large order being shipped out on the last train to Oro, a small town like Wycliff, some four hours southeast. Micah diligently gathered everything needed for the order, keeping himself far too busy to talk about the events of the night before. I took it as a clear sign last night had been a mistake, one we would both chalk up to foolishness taken too far.

When the sun dipped low, Micah hauled the order and the kids back to town, giving me only a slight tip of his head in greeting and goodbye.

So I was rather slack-jawed when I spotted Etienne and his rider coming down the dirt road only a few hours after they had gone.

I stood on the porch, hands in my apron, as Micah dropped a pack on the creaking wooden steps.

"What—" I began, mind reeling with the possibilities as to why he had returned.

"I'm staying with you tonight," he said, a bit breathless, as if he had run instead of riding his horse to get here.

A strangled laugh escaped my lips. "Don't be silly. Go home, Micah." I reached for his bag, intending to hand it back to him.

He caught my wrist, forcing me to look up at him. His face was darker from hours in the fields, hair lighter and unruly around his face. My throat was dry as I thought of my legs around his hips the night before.

"I'm staying," he said with a firmness that should have made me frown, but instead I softened, like butter left out in the sun.

"Okay," I relented, more relieved than I knew how to convey at having someone, anyone else in the house with me, but more at ease because it was Micah. I bit the inside of my cheek, forcing back the tears threatening my eyes. I didn't want him to see how badly everything was getting to me. Regardless of the weird tension between us, Micah would always keep me safe.

"You can stay in Theo's room?" I asked as if there were any other option.

"Naturally."

His mood shifted to the lighthearted, easy demeanor Micah was well known for. "I'm going to finish loading up the wagon for tomorrow's orders." He grabbed his bag and tossed it inside the front door, which I left open behind me.

"Want some help?"

He turned and stretched his arms over his head, biceps flexing.

By the Strings, what was I thinking? We were going to be in the house, together. Alone. With those biceps.

I looked away, my face warming.

"No, I want you to go inside and eat something."

"I ate," I protested. It wasn't an actual lie, I *had* eaten, it had just been six or seven hours ago from what I recalled. I glowered up at him as he beamed his signature easy smile.

"I'm serious, I will question you when I get inside." He gave me a gentle push towards the house before walking to the barn.

Deciding I could use a few minutes alone, I took the chance to go inside and panic about Micah staying over.

He was staying out of kindness, protectiveness, concern, nothing more. He didn't see me that way. But what if he did? What if he leaned in to kiss me or something else, something more? We would be alone together, after all. What would I do? Fantasies raced through my mind faster than I had time to process. I had liked Micah for years. He was my best friend; in a way, he was family. I think somewhere along the way our families had even begun expecting us to end up together. I had been waiting for that day, expecting it myself. It seemed inevitable. Now that it might actually be happening, what did it mean? Was I ready?

To appease Micah's request, I made a chicken sandwich, but the idea of sitting inside to eat alone had me shuffling back outside to sit on the porch steps. I balanced my meager plate of food on my knees. Eyeing the sandwich, I took a small bite. The food tasted sour in my mouth, but I forced myself to swallow. The food wasn't bad. I just had no desire to eat it. Sighing, I chewed miserably, sliding the plate to the step next to me.

Faint purring reached my ears, and I looked up. The beautiful cat had returned. I had not seen the large cat since that morning, and I'd assumed, wild as he was, that he had moved on. Slowly he made his way over to me. His dark nose sniffed the air curiously. The smile that lifted my cheeks was as easy as Micah's signature grin.

"Well hello, friend," I cooed, pulling some chicken from my plate. "Hungry?" He gave a small mew unbefitting his size as he bounded up to me. I held the chicken out, and he nipped at it, pulling it from my hand. Chewing, he came closer.

"Where did you come from?" I asked as he eyed me and then the plate. I chuckled. "Okay, you can have it." I moved the bread out of the way and held the plate out to him. His ears twitched back, and he moved his head side to side. I marveled again. Even though this was the second time I had seen him use such a human gesture, my mouth still hung open; dumbstruck like the first time.

Tentatively, he pushed his head against the bottom of the plate, nudging it back towards me. I mused at his humanlike comprehension. "You want me to eat it?" I asked.

Dark eyes stared at me.

"Oh... kay..." I took a hesitant bite and forced myself to swallow again. I would not be able to finish it no matter how many bites I forced down. "Why don't we share." I separated the bread and chicken. I placed the plate of chicken on the ground in front of him and held up the bread. "I'll eat this, you eat that." I pointed from the bread to the plate. His head tilted to the side, almost deliberating.

I took a bite of bread to prove my point.

He knelt and quickly polished off the plate. I watched him. Where had he come from?

"Will you be sticking around?" I asked.

He glanced up at me, his tail twitching.

"It's because of the chicken, right?" I joked, laughing to myself. His ears tilted towards the sound as if it pleased him. "Well, in that case, I think you need a name."

His pink tongue popped out, wiping the sides of his mouth.

"What to call you... hmm..." I gazed at his silver fur. "Silver?" I proposed.

His ears flattened, and he growled.

"Okay, okay, not Silver..."

He sat back on his haunches, waiting.

"Hmmm." I ran through some names, nothing sounding quite right.

His head tilted, eyes reflecting the porch light. They flashed, like two coins catching the sun. It should have been terrifying, but the iridescent glint only made him seem more mysterious.

I clapped my hands together. "I've got it! I'll call you Iri." He dropped his head, peering up at me almost warily. "Do you not like it? Iri, for your eyes. They do this iridescent thing. I like it." I nodded, proud of myself.

His ears shifted front and back as his head turned towards the barn. Micah's dark figure approached the house. Iri rose, drawing my attention. He stared into my eyes, giving me pause. What was he trying to tell me?

I could hear Micah's boots in the dirt only a few paces off. My brow furrowed as Iri backed away.

"Hey, Micah." I waved. "You finished?"

"Yeah," he called.

I rose to my feet, dusting off my apron.

Iri moved in front of me, teeth bared at Micah.

"Hey, no, it's okay, Micah is a friend." I pet Iri behind the ear, willing him to calm down. His eyes did not leave Micah's approaching form.

"I told you to eat, not feed stray cats." Micah smiled, finally reaching us. He paused, taking in Iri with a curious gaze.

"I ate."

"Uh-huh." He nodded to the plate in my hand. "Let's get inside, it's too cold to be sitting out here." Micah rubbed his arms, walking up the steps and inside. "Big cat," Micah observed as he moved past Iri.

"I know, right?" I agreed, turning to follow him. Iri rubbed past my legs, slipping through the front door.

I supposed Micah and I would not be as alone as I had originally thought.

CHAPTER 8

Had Me In The Palm Of Your Hand

Once inside, all the fears and nightmares surfaced in my mind. I had completely forgotten my distress while I was with Iri.

Closing the door, I locked it with a definite *click*. I breathed a sigh and moved through the house, checking the locks on all the windows, checking rooms and closing doors as was quickly becoming my nightly routine. Micah followed silently behind me, watching skeptically.

Finishing my inspection of the second floor, I walked down the stairs and flopped onto the lounge.

"Had a break-in recently?" Micah queried, reclining next to me. Iri lay with eyes closed across the chaise, his large body taking up the whole thing, leaving only the space directly beside me for Micah to sit.

"No, no." I sighed, closing my eyes. "I'm just being precautious. I am a girl living alone, after all." I opened my eyes to see his expression.

"Wanna listen to the radio?" His face and tone were unreadable.

"Sure."

He flipped through the stations, stopping on some instrumental music; his signal that he actually wanted to talk.

"So have you caught up on your homework?"

"A bit, I still have that history paper to write." I had been focusing on my other subjects, worried the history lessons might encourage stranger dreams with the peculiar speculations. "Honestly I'm not sure I'll be able to keep up with the assignments this year." I fiddled with a loose string on my sweater.

"I'm always available to help," he offered. "Wanna work on something now?"

"Oh, umm." I didn't really want to do homework in case I woke up again in the middle of the night; I would need something to do like last night.

Micah lifted his bag from the floor and pulled out the purple-and-orange history book.

"Most of it is pretty redundant from previous years, but there is one part that seemed interesting." He shifted close, laying the book on his lap, his arm going around the back of the lounge behind my head. Our sides were flush against each other. If he noticed or did it intentionally, it clearly was not affecting him as much as it was me.

I eyed the book nervously. My palms started to sweat.

He opened it, flipping through the pages till he found what he was looking for.

"Here it is." His breath tickled the top of my head as he showed me the passage in the book. "In the 3,800th year of King Roark's reign, the queen was killed by Skithian in an attempt to end the bloodline. However, some say that before she died she bore a son," he read. "Very little is known about this, and it is all considered speculation, as only two hundred years later the king also died and peace began."

"A prince?" I asked, confused. "If there really was a prince, why hasn't he taken back the throne?" When King Roark died, the court had appointed the steward to the throne. The steward has reigned for the last two hundred years.

Micah looked at me, his confusion mirroring my own. "You have never heard of a prince either?"

"No, why would I have? It hasn't been in history books till now, apparently," I answered, furrowing my brow. It was odd that this little piece of information had never been shared with the public. So why now? "It's silly for them to add it now. If he were alive, real, he would have ascended to the throne when the war began again fifty years ago. The steward is super old, even for someone in the King's Court." Those in the king's inner circle, including the king himself, were given abnormally long life by the Creator of Strings. "Besides," I continued, "who knows if the court even has a plan for when he passes."

"I'm sure someone has a plan," Micah said, sounding as discouraged as I felt.

I didn't want to talk about the royal family anymore, it only made me think of the war and thus of Father and Theo.

"I'm pretty tired," I lied, forcing a yawn to prove my point.

"Oh?" He looked surprised. It was still pretty early. "Of course, we should go to bed," he agreed, then repositioned next to me as if finally realizing how much of our bodies were touching.

"Micah, thank you for staying here," I said sheepishly, turning my head to look up at him.

"Anytime." He smiled, though I could tell he was confused and maybe even a little disappointed. I would have shown more interest in the conversation in the past.

"Sorry, we can talk about it more another time," I amended, feeling guilty for lying. He gave me his easy smile and dropped his hand onto my shoulder, drawing me into a hug. My body twisted into him on the lounge. My heart pounded in my chest as my cheek rested on his collarbone.

He took a deep breath. "Haya." He said my name like a swear, like a plea. It sounded good. It seemed powerful somehow. It made me bold.

I tilted my head up, lips brushing the warm golden skin at the base of his throat. My braid fell back over my shoulder as I shifted, brazen in my attempt to get him to whisper my name again. Was his heart pounding as hard as mine was? Was he aware of how badly I wanted to kiss him? My hands gripped his shoulders as I pushed up, straddling his legs as I had the night before, this time with intention. I would not let this time be mistaken for an accident. I was done with my one-sided crush. Done waiting for him to make the first move. I had loved Micah for years, and I couldn't let this opportunity pass, even if it turned out to be a terrible choice.

I had never done anything like this before, and a part of me wanted reassurance that I wasn't doing it wrong, but if I wavered now, Micah would turn it into some kind of joke.

"Haya."

My pulse jumped as his tone took on a warning edge. I lifted my eyes to his as I settled down onto his lap. His hands slid down my sides, settling on my hips. I gasped at the contact. No touch had ever been so deliciously shocking. I wanted to feel it again.

"By the Strings, who taught you to do this?" Micah

groaned, and the most intoxicating thing happened as he spoke. His pupils dilated, nearly inking out his chestnut eyes.

Despite myself I asked, "A-Am I doing it wrong?" I shifted my hips, unsure if it was uncomfortable for him.

"By the Strings," he swore, "stop moving." He released my hips, hands covering his face. Panic fluttered in my chest.

"I-I'm sorry."

"Don't. Don't." He exhaled, leaning his head back, hands still covering his face. "Armond and Theo would absolutely kill me," he mumbled behind his hands.

My brow furrowed. Why was he talking about my father and brother at a time like this?

"I don't understand."

"No, of course you wouldn't, that's something I love about you."

My face grew hard; somehow it didn't seem like a compliment. I scrambled off his lap and stood. I noticed then Iri was no longer on the chaise. Where had the cat gone?

Micah seemed to relax immensely now that I was no longer plastered to his body. It was hard not to take offense to the obvious discomfort he felt at my touch.

"Haya, I'm not—" He opened his eyes. "I should have been, but I'm not prepared to have this conversation with you yet."

He was rejecting me? It was as if he had the vibration gift and shoved a powered punch right through my gut. He didn't know how to let me down, how to tell me he only saw me as a kid sister, just like Theo.

Heat burned my cheeks.

"Good night, then," I said in a rush, and bolted upstairs. I closed the door to my room as hot embarrassed tears filled my eyes. Numbly I followed my nightly routine, brushing my teeth, dressing in my nightgown and rebraiding my hair, all the while replaying my foolishness over and over again. The furrow in my brow seemed like it could be a new permanent fixture on my face as I curled into a fetal position, pulling my blanket over my head.

Micah's steps stopped in front of my door.

"Haya?" he called softly, but I squeezed my eyes shut, willing him to go away. After a prolonged silence he sighed. "Sweet dreams."

How ironic. My dreams had not been sweet for weeks, and the one sweet dream I'd had was walking down the hall to my brother's room, turning into a nightmare that could rival the ones in my sleep. Or so I had thought until that night's nightmare began.

———

The moon was full overhead and the valley cold; a light frost dusted the ground. I was running through the wheat in my nightgown. The dreams always seemed to start with me running. The world was dark, the path through the stalks the only thing clear through my eyes. My nightgown caught on the wheat stalks. I could feel the shadows watching me, peering at me between the slender growth as I ran. I listened to my breathing, trying to find my way out of the field. I rubbed my eyes with the back of my hands, trying to better my sight. A dark arm reached out to me, grasping. Most of my senses were diminished. I couldn't see well, hear well or feel the ground beneath my feet. So, the fire that burned my arm where the creature clawed at me was petrifying. I cried out in agony and twisted to get free. Even free of the smoky dark mass, my skin sizzled, making me queasy. I pushed through the break in the wheat in front of the barn. I fumbled with the sliding door, opening it enough to stumble in. I latched the door shut and took in the darkness of my surroundings. My arm flared again as my eyes adjusted. This was the wrong place to run. The faint moonlight turned a pale crimson. Shadows slipped around my ankles, holding me in places as I sank into the mud. The cold air filling my lungs as the contrast of the fire on my skin confused my weak senses. I was trapped, I could not move. Tears of helplessness rolled from the corners of my eyes.

"Please..." My voice broke as I tried to breathe. "... help me." I choked as the last of my breath was taken. My eyes fell closed. I knew I was dreaming, but the pain, the lack of air, felt so real. My skin suffered like being stung by thousands of bees. The fire bubbled in my throat like I was drowning in boiling water. I was really dying.

My body became weightless, and for a moment I was sure I was dead, floating on to the afterlife. My eyes opened as firm arms held tightly around me. My senses cleared, and I could feel, hear, see and even taste everything. The air smelled of mint and cedar. Arms wrapped under my legs and back, holding me tight. The embrace was so rigid I couldn't move at all.

The barn door was slightly ajar, a pale purple light illuminating the space around me. I lifted my hand to cover my eyes and peered up to see who was holding me. I could feel the dream slipping around me with each step the stranger took towards the pale light.

"Am I dead?" I whispered, my lips feeling detached from my body.

Everything moved in slow motion, and I could hear my name being called faintly in the back of my mind. I squinted up to see dark brown hair hanging down past a strong jaw, and the curve of a full lip, which appeared to be moving. Was he speaking to me? I could not hear any words, but it seemed to match the sound in my head. He looked down at me, light illuminating his strong angled face, long thick lashes framing dark eyes. Though dark, his eyes reflected the light, making them flash iridescent. His face was young, but his eyes resonated more than one lifetime in their deep pools. He was without a doubt the most beautiful person I had ever seen. Then he smiled, and my heart danced out of my chest and into reality.

I sat up with a start, feeling the emptiness around my body where his arms had folded me up. Movement beside me caused me to scream and press back into the wall.

"It's just me," Micah said quickly, reaching out to hold my shoulders.

"What-t?" My teeth chattered as I trembled. My eyes were wet, and my whole body was hot but covered in gooseflesh.

"Haya, you were screaming." I jumped again at Micah's voice. "Are you okay?" he pressed, tilting his head to get a better look at me.

"Micah..." I breathed, searching his eyes for something to ground myself. "Y-You startled me." The dream was still wrapped around me, even if his arms were not. The dream coaxed me like the melody of a song you can't remember the words to.

Was he some kind of spirit?

His eyes. They were so familiar. I squeezed my own eyes shut, trying to keep the image in my consciousness a few moments longer. I wanted to go back to the dream and see his face once more. I tried to carve every detail into my memory, but even in the few seconds I had been awake, the details had become hazy.

"Haya?"

"Sorry, Micah." I opened my eyes. "I didn't mean to wake you." Coming completely back to myself, I relaxed my shoulders. It was just a dream. *He* was just a dream.

"That's hardly the issue here," he said, aggravated. "How long have you been having nightmares like that?"

"It's nothing." I pushed him away, getting out of bed. The room was suddenly too stuffy. I left down the stairs and out the front door. Micah was quick to follow me, joining me on the porch.

The night sky was brightened by the full moon. The light bathed the swaying wheat in a silver glow, reminding me of something I couldn't place.

"I hate it when girls say that. It's definitely *not* nothing," he said, stopping me on the porch steps. Hand on my shoulder, he guided me to sit. "I live with two women, remember?"

"Over a week," I relented, answering his question and sitting next to him. "They are all different." I dropped my head into my hands as if I could hold my mind together from the outside. My fingers threaded in the tangles of my hair. My braid must have unfurled in my sleep. I was a mess, my thin nightgown slipping off my shoulder and riding up my thighs.

Micah had never seen me like this, even though this was not the first time he had stayed overnight. Theo would often have sleepovers, but I was always careful to make sure I was presentable. Despite his obvious rejection earlier, my face warmed with embarrassment at my state of undress. Not that it was probably appealing to him—I was sure I looked like the death I had experienced in the dream. Still, I tried to pat down the stray hairs and discreetly wipe my face of any drool. It was superficial, but I had to do something when he was sitting there looking perfectly unruffled by sleep. His pants and shirt were only slightly unkempt with wrinkles, his hair a wonderfully wild mess of gold.

"Why didn't you tell me or my mom? If you were having such a hard time, we would not have left you alone so much." His voice was softer but still obviously annoyed.

"I don't want to be a burden; besides, you have a lot of other things to deal with, taking on all the sales and order fulfillment. I'm practically an adult. I can handle some silly nightmares." I tried to laugh, but it came out like a wheeze. The night was cold, and my breath turned to white wisps.

"By the look on your face, they don't seem like silly nightmares. They look to be a lot more than that. Can you tell me what happened?"

"The first one was a dream that the whole farm was burning and that Theo and Father were dead. Everyone was. Then... then they got worse." I closed my eyes again.

"Worse? I can't imagine what's worse than losing your family." He gestured to the farm. "Your whole life. Even in a dream, that's a lot to process."

I softened at his understanding. Micah had always been like this. Theo and I never really saw eye to eye on things, but Micah just seemed to understand me in a way not even my family could.

"You have had a lot to deal with lately," Micah continued. "Your mind is just trying to understand everything going on." He rubbed my back. The same way my mother might have if she were here.

"I keep telling myself that. That they are just dreams, but *nothing* about these dreams feels like my imagination. They are so *so* real." I shivered, recalling the feel of burns on my flesh, the fear of not getting enough air. The hairs on the back of my neck rose as if the shadows were still, even now, waiting, observing their next chance to strike. Even during the day, I was uneasy. Even with people around, the sun shining, I felt unsafe. Something had changed on an unseeable level.

Nothing was the same. Nothing was safe.

Not only had my life changed outwardly in the last few weeks, months even, but I'd changed inside too. My responsibilities on the farm had become a burden, something they never were before. I wasn't content. I wasn't accepting my lot. I had never wished for the gift after my father's fight with his friend, but now I desperately wished for it. I would have never come on to Micah like I had earlier. The changes were subtle and almost imperceptible; if it weren't for the asphyxiating trepidation of being stalked, I might not have connected them at all. Moreover, this paranoia in my daily life was making me physically sick. Starved and sleep deprived.

"I feel like I'm being watched all the time." I choked a sob down, letting the confession ring in my ears, searching for any falsehood in it. I found none.

"By who?" Micah asked, scanning the fields as if he could find the stalker in our midst.

"I don't know, I sound completely crazy!" I gripped my head harder. "I live on a farm in the middle of nowhere." I threw my arms out, gesturing at the sleepy farm. My rational conviction burst forth as if it were a tangible thing. "No one is watching me. It's just... these things in my dreams keep pursuing me. I know it's irrational, but I feel so exposed everywhere." I wrapped my arms around my torso. The cold was prickling my skin, but it wasn't the main reason I was cold. No, the cold hand of death had touched me in my dream, and I would not be able to shake that, not for a long time.

"The only person watching you is me," Micah mumbled, catching me off guard.

"W-What?" I paused, catching his attempt to lighten the mood. I closed my eyes, sighing gratefully, and took the out he provided. "*You* sound like a stalker," I joked, my heart skipping a little at his peculiar confession.

He gazed up at the bright night stars, letting out a sigh of his own as if I had somehow misunderstood him. "You know your family has practically adopted me." I waited, not sure where he was going. "My mom already sees you as a daughter. We know each other. Like a brother knows a sister. We have been the best of friends for a long time." He paused as if this should make sense to me; as if his meaning were clear. I swallowed, keeping the words in my heart down.

"You *are* almost an adult, but I have been one for what feels like a very long time. Since Dad died. I know I can take care of you. I think... that is what your family would want. What your father and Theo would have wanted." He smiled tentatively at me. I didn't like hearing them talked about in the past tease. "Theo already told me that I better marry you," he added with a chuckle. I looked him in the eyes, mine wide with surprise.

"What?" The rebellious word leapt free before I could breathe it back down.

"Haya, let me take care of you. You don't have to be alone on this farm. We can get married and continue on as we have been." He gestured out with his arms. "We don't have to rush things, but I don't want to leave you here, alone. I had hinted my plans to Theo and your father before they left and planned to ask officially when they got back from service, when you were older but..." He paused. "If they don't come back, I don't want you and your mother to be without support." We sat there staring at each other, my heartbeat racing away. I knew I needed to say something. I wanted to say something, I just didn't know where to start.

All I had wanted was a first kiss, for my first love to be recognized, perhaps reciprocated. Instead I got a marriage proposal.

CHAPTER 9

This Is Gonna Take Me Down

His confession left me confused. I was not sure if his admission was out of affection or out of responsibility. Was he saying all these things because he loved me, or was it a sense of camaraderie with my father and Theo that drove him to make such an audacious request? It was true our families had always anticipated we would end up together, and I guess I always thought we would too. That he would be my end, as I would be his. But the loveless revelation disturbed my heart. Sure, I had told Talie he was my crush, and he had been for so long. I cared sincerely for Micah, but had his affection towards me ever been that of lovers? To him weren't we just two people who held a deep kinship? Micah was my safety net, as Theo had been. With each passing day, my net was vanishing, and I was becoming more drawn to the comfort Micah could offer me. But was that fair to him? Would loving him for the protection he would offer me and my mother be enough?

Wouldn't he want more from his bride? I could love him with all the passion I had in me, but did he feel the same for me?

"You don't have to answer now," he said softly. "I know this is sudden, and it's the middle of the night. We should try to go back to bed." He stood, holding his hand out to help me up. I looked at his hand, the hand that, when we were children, pushed me down, waved me away saying no girls allowed, but yet threw punches for me on the playground, held out an offering with my favorite candies and carried baskets of eggs that were too heavy for me. A hand I could readily hold for a lifetime. That was who Micah was to me. His hands told a million stories about us. I slid my cold fingers into his, letting the prospect lift me out of the present suffering to a future that, perhaps, could be brighter.

"You're freezing," he chided, feeling my chilled fingers. I shivered as I stood in my nightgown.

"It's a pretty cold night," I said tightly, careful not to let my teeth chatter.

"The harvest!" He looked out over the fields. I followed his gaze, seeing a light frost on the grass.

"Oh no." I panicked, unsure what to do. In the past, Father would stay up and plow the fields, careful not to let the frosts ruin anything. But if he were here, the crops would have already been harvested and on their way to the surrounding towns by now. We would have not been so behind.

"Grab me a coat," he ordered. "I'll set up the machines and harvest what I can." I nodded, running inside to grab Theo's winter coat. Passing it to Micah, I hurried upstairs to dress in something warmer. When I came down he had already started, and I ran out to join him on the plow. We worked till the sky turned a soft gray hinting at daybreak.

"You should get some sleep." He nudged me, as I had dozed off again.

"We both should." I yawned and tried to wake up.

"I'm not the one who hasn't been sleeping for weeks. Go. Before I drag you upstairs," he threatened in good humor.

I wanted to say that didn't sound so bad but bit back my cheeky retort.

"Fine, fine." I waved and walked blearily to the house. I hauled myself up the stairs, not bothering to change my dirty clothes. I fell into my bed, curling into a ball on my side and wrapping the blanket around my still-shivering bones.

I drifted, and for once in what felt like forever I did not dream.

When I woke later, the sun was high. I had slept well past noon. Micah had left. On the dining table sat a note saying he had gone home to check on Misha, who had come down with a cold. The day passed by, and the kids came and went, and though my thoughts should have been on the proposal the night before, instead they ambled time and again to the nightmare. Most specifically to the dark-haired man who had saved me. Would I dream of him tonight? Would he come to save me again? Not that I wanted a reason to be saved. I would be just fine never dreaming of those monsters again. But something told me they would not be easily removed from my sleep. Maybe the man who'd saved me could keep those evil shadows from creeping into my dreams altogether. When he had appeared, it was like the atmosphere of my whole dream had changed. Not only did those *things* vanish and my senses sharpen—I had sensed how real the dream was

—but when he touched me, it was no different than when Micah had grabbed my shoulders after I woke. Was that even possible? I was pretty sure it wasn't. In those few moments, we, the man and I, were in sync. No. Not quite in sync, more like harmonious. We meshed together in a way I could not explain. It just was right somehow.

I pushed chicken around on my plate and flattened my potato with the back of my fork. I was seriously overthinking. "Ughhh," I groaned, dropping my fork on the table. I mean, why was I even thinking about some dream guy when a very real guy just asked me to be his?

Micah's confession was a whole other point of contention in my mind. I hadn't given him an answer, and I didn't think I would be able to—not till I was certain of his feelings for me.

I rose, putting the chicken into a small bowl. I tossed on a thick sweater and walked to the porch. Twilight greeted me. The day had reached another end, though I had only been awake for a short while.

I sat on the porch waiting for my furry friend, as I had not seen him since Micah and I were on the lounge last night.

"Iri?" I called, not really expecting him to come. To my surprise the big silver cat cavorted out of the wheat stalks. "Well, hello. Didn't expect you to still be around." I smiled as he sniffed the air. "Ahh," I teased. "You're only interested in the chicken. Fine, but first you have to listen to me."

He cocked his head, waiting. I marveled at his strange ability to comprehend me. "I have some things I need to get off my chest, and, well... I can't really talk to anyone else. Will you listen?"

As if responding to my request, he sat down at my feet, looking up expectantly. "Well..." I hesitated, feeling a little silly. "My friend. Micah. You saw him yesterday. He asked me to marry him..." His ears twitched but showed no other signs of acumen. "I don't think I can marry him. I mean, I don't know if he really wants to, that is." I reached down, scratching behind his ears and under his chin. "I love him, have for a long time, but he doesn't see me that way. He—He wants to marry me out of obligation, as protection... I think..." I sighed. "Sharing about this isn't helping after all."

Iri pushed his head against my shin.

"You're really sweet. I don't think talking about it will make a difference. I'm so mixed up in my head." I thought of the man from my dream. He was likely a figment of my imagination, but I couldn't explain why my face flushed at the thought of him. Was I boy crazy? Did this just happen to girls who were seventeen and had never been kissed? "Oh my gosh, I'm blushing, aren't I?" I touched my cheeks, appalled.

Iri cocked his head again.

"You don't see in color, sorry, I forgot." I giggled ridiculously. Mortified, I slapped my forehead as if the action could will my brain to function better. "How do I say this... Let's say, hypothetically of course, you are torn between two guys. One guy proposes, he is safe, comfortable, like family, you love him, while the other guy, a total mystery and most likely not real, saves your life. You're likely never to meet this hero, but he makes your heart race, and you have no idea why, but you can't forget about him. What do you do? Choose the safety or the one who makes you question your sanity? One will most definitely lead to pain, while the other might lead to a more subtle dissatisfaction." I paused, waiting, as if Iri could actually respond.

His dark eyes bore unblinking into mine. "I'm losing my mind... ughh!" I bunched my fingers into my hair, flinging the strands wildly until it was an unkempt mess. I sighed, leaning back onto my hands. "You're lucky you're a cat and don't have to deal with this human stuff." I took out the chicken and placed it in front of Iri. He had definitely earned the bowl and more after listening to my ramblings.

He eyed the chicken and then me, still waiting. "It's okay, eat. I should probably stop talking to animals." I leaned forward and whispered, "People might talk." I winked at him.

He blinked slowly but leaned down to eat the meat. I watched silently, mesmerized once again by the tiny prisms the sunlight was making in his fur. I scooted closer and ran my fingers lightly over him.

Iri glanced up, his eyes flashing. He had been purring softly, but at my touch it intensified.

"Where did you come from?" I whispered incredulously. "I've never seen anything like you before." I twisted a few strands of silver between my fingers. "That's not saying much, though. Maybe you're as common as any other cat." Though I doubted it. "I haven't been hardly anywhere." I frowned. It never bothered me much before. I had always been at peace on the farm; resigned to this life after the gift never manifested. That was until recently. "The farthest I've been is Tyndale, but that was a long time ago."

His dark eyes watched me carefully as I spoke.

"Are you still hungry?"

He shifted his head from side to side. I had never seen a cat reject food, especially chicken.

"Are you sick?"

He blinked, giving me a look that almost made me chagrin for asking. We sat for a few moments, his angled eyes seeming to narrow as if he was concentrating really hard.

My skin grew hot, and I swallowed uncomfortably. This

could be the moment he killed me... You just never knew with cats.

I laughed, disquieted, breaking the moment. "Ugh, well, it's been nice, but I should get to sleep." I stood, opening the door and letting us both inside.

Iri bounded up the stairs and out of sight like he knew exactly where he was going. "You have got to be kidding me..." Let a cat sleep in your bed one night and it becomes the rule rather than the exception.

I simpered as I proceeded with my nightly lockdown of the house.

When I finally went upstairs I found Iri holding my birthday present in his mouth.

"Iri! Drop it," I scolded, worried his teeth might ruin the gift I had been too heartbroken to open.

Iri dropped the wrapped golden package, the paper ripping as it hit the floor.

"No." I ran forward, falling to my knees. I reached for the purple fabric that spilled from the gold wrapping. It was the blanket my father had given Theo when he got the vibration gift. It was made of the most exceptional fabric, easily three times the value of one summer's crop. The rich color and material were not the only things that made this blanket valuable, but also the three impeccably embroidered golden stars that fanned out along the lower right corner.

It was not something Theo should have given me, as it was passed down in my family to those who had manifested the gift, and though I hadn't coveted the vibration gift, I had coveted this stunning blanket. Theo knew that and had given it to me despite our family tradition.

Tears pooled in my eyes as I gripped the blanket close to my chest.

"Thank you, Theo," I whispered.

Iri nudged the fabric in my arms.

"Thank you too, Iri. If not for your meddling, I might have never opened it," I muttered, softly scratching him behind his velvety ear.

He twitched, tail ticking at the contact.

We both crawled into bed, wrapped up in the luxurious blanket. I was surprised to find that, though I worried about the nightmares, I was strangely at ease nestled between the blanket and my meddlesome furry friend.

CHAPTER 10

Saved By A Perfect Kiss

I lay in a field of dandelions. The warm summer air filled my lungs. The clouds were big and puffy against a cool blue sky. It was late in the day. I sat up knowing that I was in a dream again. I hated how I was completely aware of the dream. At least this one didn't start with me running in terror. I could see better in this dream, and my senses were not muted as they had been before. The grass scraped my bare legs as I pulled my knees to my chest. I looked around for any shadows, but everything was light from the evening sun.

"Hello?" I called, not sure if anyone was around. I was uncomfortably alone. Absently I twisted the end of my braid between my fingers. "I-Is anyone here?" I paused, waiting.

The silence of the dream was almost palpable as my heart sank. I suppose I had really been hoping to see the strange boy, but I should have known I wouldn't dream of something so beautiful again.

Apparently I could only dream of monsters night after night. I grimaced at the thought of those dark masses converging and separating like incorporeal shades of Skithian.

As if fueled by my thoughts of them, the dream began to change. The world around me sped forward. The puffs of clouds convulsed in the sky as the sun dipped low and disappeared behind the mountains. I watched in horror as within seconds the sudden darkness was lit by a blood red moon. The hairs on the back of my neck pricked on end as the harmless tree line took on new life. Before I could think, I was up and running down the dandelion hill, slipping on the wet red that coated the once yellow and white dandelions. Blood seemed to fill my vision as the moon painted the landscape crimson. The squelching of mud and blood pressed between my toes and splashed up the hem of my nightgown.

No no no. This couldn't be happening again. I wouldn't die like this.

"What do you want from me!" I cried, stumbling down the hill, looking back at the living darkness. "Please, please leave me alone," I whimpered.

The mass shifted and swirled as an almost humanlike face pressed out of the black smoke. The empty cavity of its eyes seemed to fix on me. Its formless mouth appeared to pour out black sludge. An earsplitting screech I had not heard in any of the other dreams permeated the valley as if the land itself were crying out in agony.

I covered my ears and turned away, running as fast as I could to the gate. I kept running till I reached the dirt road that led to town. The sensation of weightlessness caused me to stop. I couldn't feel the ground under my feet. My vision became hazy as I looked around. I glanced back toward the hill, relieved to see the mass had vanished. I wiped sweat from my neck, swallowing passed the tight lump in my throat.

I still felt the strange weightlessness though my blood-soaked feet remained firmly on the ground. There was nothing to cause a shadow on the open dirt path. Or so I thought, as my own shadow rose from the ground, a smoky black mass snaking up around my legs. My eyes widened as the vapor-like face slithered up my torso, empty eyes staring. "No..." I gasped as it gripped my ankles and wrists, rooting me in place. I could not move as the smoke burned my flesh. "NO!"

The road ahead began to splinter, opening in small cracks reaching out towards my feet. My vision tunneled, my skin burning with the same fiery sensation of the last dream. I was sinking into the black mass. It was absorbing me. Sucking me down through the widening cracks in the path. As if I was breathing it in. The misty blackness wrapped around my middle, burning holes into my gown. The sting became excruciating, like my ribs were breaking under the black fire. "Please... someone... h-help me..." My vision speckled gray as panic scrambled any last coherent thoughts. I could no longer tell if the ground had swallowed me whole or if I was still standing. My mind screamed, telling me to grab anything. To simply hold on. I tried to stretch my arms out but only felt the fire, the boiling black water that filled my lungs.

My fingers strained. My breathing labored as I had the faintest sensation of falling backwards. But when I would have expected to hit the ground, I did not.

Light exploded around me, causing me to open my closed eyes. I squinted, confused by the luminous shine that came from nowhere in particular. It was soothing in its warmth over my skin. The two sensations of gentle warmth and excruciating burning muddled my senses further. Slowly the warmth of the light dissolved the fire.

Then my heart raced with hope. This light. Was he here? I reached my arms blindly about, recoiling when strong arms wrapped around my waist from behind, pulling me into a solid chest.

The light softened, the world taking shape past the haze of light and smoke till my vision was clear again.

I rested my head back against his shoulder, knowing without looking that it was my savior from before.

"You came," I whispered, a strangled whimper of relief escaping my lips.

The darkness. The fire. It was all gone, but the ache of pain still pulsed along my skin. It and the burn marks around my gown were the only tangible reminders of the trauma.

I tilted my head, angling to see his face.

He was nothing like what my muddled memory had recalled. His dark eyes were more exotic, his jaw more cut, his proportions more unnaturally perfect. His golden skin seemed to glow against the rich brown tendrils that framed his face.

My memory had not done him justice.

"It's okay, you are safe now." The voice from the last dream echoed in my mind. The lips of the man moved, but no sound came from him.

I grabbed a fistful of the white shirt he wore, turning in his arms, and I crushed my face into his strong chest. When had tears begun streaming down my cheeks?

He stiffened but let me cling to him as sobs racked through me. "It's okay. You're okay," he soothed. The smell of cedar and mint filled my nose, and I gripped him tighter.

He wrapped his arm gently around my shoulders, as if I were a dandelion and one rough move would scatter me into pieces.

I wanted to stay right here. I didn't care if those things ever came back, because I knew right here I was safe. Right here nothing bad could touch me. I never wanted to leave his arms.

I did not want to face waking up from this moment, this dream. The wholeness I experienced in this spirit's arms almost made facing those monsters worth it. It was like nothing bad could ever touch me again.

We lingered like that for a long time. Until the strangled noises quivering from my lips turned into silent tears. I didn't move even when it seemed like he was ready to pull away. I clasped on to him. Hugging him so hard I thought I might have been hurting him, but truthfully I didn't care if I was.

I could feel the steady rise and fall of his chest. I could hear the rhythmic beat of his heart echoing my own. Slowly I opened my eyes. Our feet were planted on the ground atop the dandelion hill, my toes unmarred by blood and dirt. I looked around; the sun was bright overhead, all traces of night and the red moon gone.

My savior looked down at me with a steady, familiar gaze.

He's not real, I reminded myself. He could not be real?

I had been so sure before that I had been dying. Positive it was real, but now my brain fought that logic. I could clearly hear the sound of his heartbeat moments ago. Why was it easier to believe the nightmare to be real and this fantasy a farce?

This had to be a dream. I hadn't really been dying.

His hands moved to hold my shoulders as he pulled back from our embrace.

"Are you okay?" the voice in my head asked while his lips moved. Confused, I put my hand to my head. I had not imagined it in the last dream. He was speaking to me but in my mind.

"How is that..." Possible? I tilted my head. I knew I could

hear, I had just heard his heartbeat, so why could I not hear his voice? "How are you doing that?" I asked, brow furrowed.

He looked startled for a moment. Something flashed in his dark eyes as a slow smile spread across his face.

"You can hear me?" his voice said again; this time his lips did not move.

"Yes." I raised my eyebrows, feeling more sure this was all just a dream. People couldn't speak to other people's minds. "Though it's a bit unnerving." I shifted my weight, all too aware of his heavy hands on my shoulders. "Why can't I just have you talk normal?" I complained to myself.

"What?" He shook his head, then understanding dawned across his features. "T-This is not a dream. Do you think this is a dream?" he asked, incredulous.

I flinched back out of his grip. How had he known I was struggling with that conclusion? Of course this was a dream. There was no other explanation, plus I knew I was sleeping.

"You can't control anything outside of yourself here. You can't control me, just like you couldn't control the Wraiths." He bit his lip as if it had been his lips that said something they shouldn't have. He swallowed, taking a small step towards me.

I stepped back, distrust filling me even as the blue sky and green grass spotted with white dandelions seemed to be enticing me to trust. My intuition tugged me towards him, telling me he was safe. To trust him.

"I'm getting ahead of myself. Erm, where to start... Ugh, I can't keep making mistakes. I knew she was the one to help me but..." He looked wide-eyed at me and backed away a little as if I was the one scaring him and not the other way around.

We had shuffled in this awkward dance so much so that we stood at a more prudent distance from one another. We were no longer two people who had just shared an embrace moments ago. We were strangers.

He rubbed the back of his neck. "You could hear all of that..." He frowned. It wasn't a question.

Before he could start speaking again in my head, I jumped in. "This is my dream," I insisted.

"I'm sorry, I need to focus better so I don't confuse you." His voice flooded my mind, and I clamped my hands over my ears as if this simple act could shut him out. I glared at his beautiful face. I wanted to wake up. I didn't want to dream anymore. Unease was building in me, and I couldn't place why. He wasn't hurting me. He had saved me. Yet, I could not ignore the distress turning in my chest.

"S-Stop..." I held up my hands defensively. "The talking in my head, it's..." I paused, looking for a word, "I don't like it." It was too invasive. Unconsciously I wrapped my arms around my body, feeling exposed.

I was overreacting. It wasn't like he was reading my thoughts. That would have been more perturbing. "I know you're a dream," I said softly. "Still..." I could not deny the inexplicable connection I had to this boy. I had felt it in the last dream too. "This is... I don't know how to say it... not normal. I shouldn't know I'm dreaming." I breathed out.

He appeared frustrated as he ran his fingers through his dark locks, jaw twitching as he sighed through his teeth. Grabbing my forearms, he pulled my arms away from my body and drew me to sit on the ground. The blades of grass were scratchy along my bare legs.

Eyes serious, he said my name, his tone almost a warning. "Haya."

I swallowed. "How do you know my name?"

"Please listen to me, please listen to everything I'm going

to say, even if it is uncomfortable or doesn't make sense. Can you do that?"

Panicked by the intensity of his request and equally confused by it I stammered, "T-Thank you for saving me from the... what did you call them?"

"Wraiths."

I laughed without humor. "The things my mind has been conjuring up lately are just horrible."

He stared blankly at me, dropping my forearms.

"You have no idea what is going on," he said, his voice faint in my head, as if he was talking to himself.

"I'm dreaming," I affirmed, annoyed. "I guess, maybe, on some level this is my subconscious or something." I shrugged. My free hands traced the bumps in my braid as I realized suddenly that my nightgown was wholly intact, the blood stains gone as if the encounter with the Wraiths hadn't happened. Even the dull ache where I had been burned had faded. It hadn't been real.

"Haya." He grabbed my shoulders, and I peered up, startled.

"Yes?" I asked, sure he was just a figment of my imagination after all.

"I'm not a figment of your imagination."

I flinched as if slapped.

"Did you just—"

"My name is Shroding," he said quickly, then hesitated. His voice in my head seemed scrambled, as if he couldn't decide on what words to use. "Can you listen to everything I'm about to say, as a thank you for saving you?" he bargained, jaw clenched. "It's more like the fourth time I've saved you, but who's counting."

My lips formed a small O.

"You heard that too? By the Strings, this is more difficult than I expected."

"I don't understand." I shook my head, feeling like it was about to burst. My imagination had a name?

I squeezed my eyes shut. Adrenaline quickened my heartbeat, and my legs itched to stand. Itched to run.

Sensing my desire to bolt, Shroding pressed down on my shoulders, firmly rooting me in place.

"Please," he begged, desperation in his voice. "You're in danger. Your dreams are not actually dreams. Each night when you feel like you are dying... it is real. In your bed, you are dying. Each night it will get worse until they get what they want."

I almost couldn't hear his words past the blood pulsing in my ears. I had almost died?

"What do they want?" I asked, my voice small.

"Us. Dead."

Dead. It didn't make sense. Wraiths—he had called the black smoke Wraiths. Why did they want me dead?

He watched me, his dark eyes steady, waiting.

I blinked. He was crazy. Absolutely crazy. Gorgeous and crazy. Or was I crazy? I was nauseous with confusion. His hands fisted on my shoulders; he was clearly displeased with my reaction.

"Are you at least familiar with Shamar's history?" he asked, trying to keep his tone gentle, but he looked upset.

All I could do was nod.

"The southern kingdom of Golan?" he continued. I nodded again. "Wraiths are the souls of those who die from vibration sickness," he explained. "Do you know what vibration sickness is?" His tone was impatient.

I had heard stories about the soldiers from the southern

kingdom. They had found a way to twist the gift to gain more power. The practice was forbidden in Shamar as it made those who succumb to the temptation monsters. Mindless beasts. Vibration sickness was caused when a person inflicted continuous use of their vibration gift on their own flesh, allowing them to withstand longer use of their powers in battle. But the side effects were horrendous. Their flesh, after a while, would no longer stay attached to their bones. They became people who looked like they were slowly disintegrating. Decaying like a corpse. The vibrations separated skin from bone, muscle from tissue, all splitting apart. The constant abuse of their power overtime caused their brain to stop working, as the vibrations eventually caused an aneurysm. The brain could only take so much repeated trauma. It was a sad way to live and an even worse way to die. They were soldiers till their last breath. Mindless monsters of their own making.

"You are not being pursued by just any Wraiths. These are the original ones from when Skithian was in power. Maybe at first it was the lesser ones, but I'm sure you've noticed things getting worse the last few days."

I nodded weakly.

"It's partially my fault." He looked chagrined. "When I showed up I made things more complicated. They know you are important, and not just because you have a strong vibration ability, but—"

"I don't," I interrupted. "I don't have a vibration gift. It never manifested when I was fifteen. There is some mistake. Those things don't want me dead. I'm nobody. All of this is impossible."

It was absurd, everything he was saying. I wanted to wake up. I didn't want to sleep anymore. I shrugged off his hold, standing, and yanked the end of my braid repeatedly as I ran down the hill.

Wake up! Wake up! Wake UP! I hit the sides of my head, trying to will myself to wake.

He ran after me, grabbing my wrist and twisting me to face him. "I can only protect you if you let me." The acute sadness in his next words took me by surprise, "Don't run from this, I can't protect you if you don't call out to me. I promise I will come every time. I won't let them hurt you." The desperate look returned to his dark eyes.

My mind reeled at his words. I fought against reason and tried hard to really hear his words. Me dying, not in the dreams but in reality. How, how could that be? How was that possible? I struggled to break his grip on my wrists. He released me, his arms falling to his sides as if resigned to let me go. I turned and began pacing, twisting the end of my braid between my fingers. It seemed real when I was being attacked, and though I didn't want to admit it, he appeared to be pretty real too. His warmth. His smell. But I remembered going to sleep.

Normally in dreams, even if you are conscious of the fact that you are dreaming, you don't have very much control, and if you do, it is hazy; things jumping, pictures and pieces that don't make sense. I was not a dream expert, but I had read a few books on the topic. I could not deny that all my dreams had been fluid, each piece progressing naturally, except for him. He'd only showed up the last two times when I called for help. So could he be telling the truth? Was this all real somehow? If it wasn't a dream, then what was it? Where was I?

I eyed him cautiously. He had sat down in the grass, giving me a moment. His legs stretched out as he leaned back on his arms. I paced a few more steps, looking around at the world. As my eyes fixed on different things, the fuzzy edges of the dream sharpened. Out of the corner of my eye I could tell he was completely in focus. He was too sharp, too real for the space we were in. Even my own body was frayed at the edges until I focused on something: my hands, hair, knees, toes. Yet he remained crystal clear. I stared unabashedly at him from top to bottom and back.

He simply watched me, as if waiting for something to click into place in my mind.

Whatever it was he was waiting for, I was pretty sure I would disappoint. I focused on his eyes, a deep brown, almost black if not for the strange flecks of gold that seemed almost iridescent. Dark brown locks hung in tousled waves to his shoulders, a style in fashion hundreds of years ago. His physique was built, strong, but not bulky. Lean muscle made for speed not brute force.

Slowly I knelt to his level, getting much closer than I would have to a real stranger. I scrutinized his eyes, trying to assess the truth in them.

"I'm not saying I believe you, but if this is not a dream, then what is it? Where am I?"

He smirked. "Now that is an excellent question," he praised. I tried to ignore the swell of pride in my chest at the compliment. "You are in a pocket dimension, much like the vibration dimension or the dimension you live life in normally. This pocket was constructed for me, and when you call out to me, the pocket I'm in is able to connect to where you are."

What in the Strings was he talking about? I perhaps should have paid better attention to the lessons Theo talked about when he first started training the gift. I think he mentioned something about the vibration dimension once, but

I hadn't paid it any mind as I did not have the gift. Was what this man was saying even possible? A pocket dimension?

I narrowed my eyes, trying to think of a way he could prove to me that this was not a dream. I had thought asking him the question would be enough, but I was even more unconvinced. How could I move between dimensions if I didn't have the vibration gift?

No—explanations, words were not enough to prove anything to me. I needed proof I could comprehend. Slowly an outrageous idea took root. By nature I was not an impulsive person, but something about the steady look in his eyes and the confusing wash of emotion coursing through me made the idea too good to pass up.

If he was a dream, then kissing him would mean nothing, be nothing. Maybe instead of saying strange things like I was dying—which I assumed was probably just my subconscious dealing with the fears for my dad and brother—this could be a different kind of dream. However, if, like he said, he was real, then I would be sacrificing my first kiss to the strange man. My thoughts briefly shifted to Micah. This kiss would not be real, I was more than certain about that fact, so it would be okay. My first kiss would still be with Micah if I accepted his hand.

I blinked hard, forcing those thoughts away.

I scooted even closer to him, resolved in my choice, ignoring the wary look in his eye as he tried to shift away from my advance.

"Kiss me," I said simply, as if it were the most natural progression to our conversation. "If you're real, prove it by kissing me."

CHAPTER 11

How Thick Do You Want This

"This"—he gestured with a hand—"is not that kind of 'dream.'" He scoffed, eyes smoldering. "This is not a dream at all." He threw his hands up, exasperated, then dropped them, fisting the ground, all pretense of patience gone. "I tell you you're in danger and dying, and you ask me to kiss you?" His tone was incredulous even as he swallowed audibly and clenched his jaw, biting back more words. I could hear the rush of them in my head, fast and unintelligible. It was hard to think with his voice running through my mind.

"No, I mean... just kiss me, okay?" I said, shaking my head as if he hadn't heard me correctly.

To my surprise, his shoulders relaxed.

"Fine, but how will it help you know I'm real?" He leaned in, closing the space between us, our lips a breath apart, as if testing my resolve.

I didn't shy away. "I'll know."

Gently, despite the reproach in his eyes, he grabbed my hand and put it to his cheek. His skin was warm.

"Is this not proof enough that I am real?" he whispered,

and I could scarcely breathe at his nearness. "Or this." He pressed his palm into the small of my back, pulling me in till I was kneeling on the ground between his legs. My heart slammed into my rib cage like a bird desperate to take flight. Still he was careful to keep our lips just far enough apart.

I swallowed hard, gripping his shoulders with both my hands to steady myself. Why was he testing me, why try and break my resolve? Did he really not want to kiss me? Perhaps I had been wrong.

All thoughts left me as his hands slid from my waist down to either side of my hips. I closed my eyes and almost whimpered.

I had never been kissed. So, a kiss was not something my subconscious could make up. In fact, the only other time I had been in this kind of situation was with Micah the other day. So these sensations were still fresh in my memory even if they were somehow way more intense with this man.

"But... I know what this feels like," I murmured, hoping he wouldn't misunderstand my meaning. It wasn't like I did this kind of thing regularly. Perhaps there was another way for him to prove his realness, but I could not deny a large part of me, larger than I would have liked to admit, wanted to know how it felt, to kiss this peculiar man—Shroding, he had called himself.

He tensed at my words, fingers pressing into my hips almost painfully. "Indeed you do. What about your proposal?"

How did he know about Micah's proposal? He could not have unless this was all in my head. More convinced that he was not real, I steeled my resolve.

I raked my hands through his dark hair, closing the distance and letting my mouth find his.

At the contact, blood rushed to my cheeks as adrenaline

made my heart dance. I was nearly undone when his soft lips parted against mine in surprise. Everything in me, my thoughts, my feelings, all seemed to fizzle out of focus till all I could feel, hear and think was him. My body trembled as a strange quivering sensation coursed through my fingers, trailing up my arms to my torso, splitting violently up and down my core. Sparks popped behind my eyes as overwhelming desire drove through me, like being plunged into ice water on a blistering hot day. I was suddenly hyperaware of everything, like for just a moment, the world stopped and I could feel all life vibrating around me. Song and color filled my ears and danced behind my eyes, and though it was painful, there was so much pleasure, so much peace and certainty in the sensations.

Shroding gasped, pulling our mouths apart.

I panted, wide-eyed. My whole body quavered in a way I did not understand. It was as if my molecules did not know how to hold together and were dispersing, and the only thing that could ground them was him.

"What have you done?" Shroding rasped, pushing me away. I flopped back onto my heels. "Your name might mean life, but I'm pretty sure you will be the death of me." He glared, clutching my upper arms, as he attempted to gather himself.

I bit my lip, rocked by his outburst and my own brazenness. What had I done?

His eyes flashed indignantly as he let me go and stood.

I needed to say something to ease the tension between us, to justify why I had kissed him, but my mind was blank, and the only thing I could reason was that I had wanted to. Shame and guilt washed over me in the aftermath of my actions.

"I-I'm so sorry. I didn't think you were real," I stammered, the guilt like a knife digging into my chest, only made worse by how good it had been. Were all kisses like that? I doubted very much he would answer that question if I asked him.

"I would ask why you did that, but I already know the answer." He worked his jaw, voice agitated in my head. I was dazed as he continued. "Are you convinced, then? Was that enough, did you get what you wanted?" His voice was rough, slicing. He was mad, very mad. "And here I thought you were some oblivious damsel in distress. Did you plan this?"

I shrunk in on myself, utterly lost. I understood him being upset, but not this angry. I had genuinely apologized, so why was he so livid? Yes, I had kissed him, certainly without his permission. I had no right to do that, and I was sorry, but how in the world had he not felt that? How had he not experienced what I had?

All I could do was blink in response, words not forming on my lips. The lips I had just used so rashly. I had just kissed this man. No qualms about it. I'd just gone for it. I was not that kind of girl. I just had my first kiss, and though I did not know what a first kiss should feel like, I was beginning to sense it didn't normally feel like that. It was right, even though it was so very wrong. And the rightness of it unhinged me. The way it made my whole being come alive was overwhelming. The way it sent my pulse pounding in my ears and warmed the whole of my body was addicting. But mostly, the way it made me want to do it again, and again, and again till my molecules were dissolved entirely and I was nothing more than dust on the wind was unnerving. I was one hundred percent sure that I would never feel like that with anyone else, and that thought out of everything was the most terrifying.

Warning bells rang in my head that this was dangerous, that I was playing with things I didn't understand, and that there would indeed be death, but not that I'd be the death of him.

As ludicrous as it was, I knew in that moment that if I let myself, I could fall in love with Shroding. This mysterious dream man that now, as he had hoped, I was convinced was real.

In his eyes, past the anger, I wondered if he had sensed it too.

I opened and closed my mouth, words feeling trapped. My hands gripped my braid and proceeded to twist the tail between my fingers. The tedious motion calmed me, my mind clearing and heart slowing to a more sustainable speed.

He had kissed me back, I was sure of it, but that fact seemed less important than what he had said before the kiss.

Shroding took three distinct breaths, fists clenched as he paced the grassy hill.

"Shroding," I whispered, using his name for the first time aloud.

He exhaled sharply, in what I hoped was relief and not exasperation.

I blinked slowly, telling myself to hear out whatever he had to say, regardless of how absurd it might sound.

"Who are you?" I asked.

He glanced in my direction, eyes narrowing, studying me for something. "You really don't know, do you? You have no idea, even though you just..." He closed his eyes and ran his hand through his hair, fingers weaving between the gentle waves. The gesture seemed to calm him somewhat. "I don't want to overwhelm you..." He paused, glancing at me. "How thick do you want this?"

I raised an eyebrow. "How thick?"

"To 'lay it on thick,' isn't that a phrase used nowadays? To overstate or exaggerate?"

What did he even mean by "nowadays"? How old was he? "Oh, um, right, then I guess lay it on me in a moderate thickness?" I smiled at the silliness of the request, but the words he spoke next were far from moderate.

He strode over and knelt on one knee, head bowed in front of me. "I am the lost Prince Shroding, prophesied to end the war with Skithian, ruler of Shesel. I have been trapped for centuries waiting to be set free so I can complete my mission, take back the throne and bring peace to the kingdoms." He raised his dark eyes to mine, piercing into my soul, my Nephesh. "And you, Haya Golden, are the only one who can set me free."

CHAPTER 12

A Call To Hope

I sat up, my vision spotting from the fast movement.

Prince Shroding. Was he somehow the son of King Roark and Queen Elina? The child speculated about in my history book?

I had never heard of a prophecy, though, and my history book only seemed concerned with the idea that a child might have been born. Nothing about what the child might do besides be the rightful king.

It was ludicrous, and yet Shroding had said he was trapped in a pocket dimension for centuries. The child of King Roark would have had to be born before the queen died some four hundred years ago. If Shroding was that child, then him being stuck in another dimension would explain why he had been gone for so long, absent from all thought and memory. It would explain why he had not taken the throne back when the war began anew. But if it were true, then that would make him four hundred years old. No one but those left from the king's court lived that long anymore, not since the king passed, but maybe I was wrong. Clearly history was wrong on a few counts.

I squeezed my eyes shut, breathing hard.

What did it all mean? Why was he coming to me?

It was impossible.

The bright afternoon sun streaked beams of gold across the floor. I planted my bare feet on the small rug next to my bed. I rubbed the woven texture between my toes and sighed.

This was real. This was my reality. This farm, Micah, the kids. Even though I did believe Shroding was somehow a real person, and perhaps he really was trapped and in need of assistance, there was no way I could possibly save him. I was just a farm girl from Wycliff.

Iri stirred on the end of the bed, his large fluffy head lifting to look at me. Somehow in the night, the purple blanket Theo had left me had wrapped around Iri, bundling him up till only his head remained visible.

I smirked.

"How did you get into such a precarious position?" I mused, crawling over to free him from the blanket bonds.

His soothing purr met my ears, and even though my body was leaden, the act of unburdening him gave me a sense of control I didn't know I needed.

"At least I'm freeing someone today." I sighed, deciding to put all thoughts of Shroding aside.

Shaking off the last dregs of sleep, I hurried through my morning routine and set to work. Work was a good distraction, for the most part. Though the night's events sat idling in my mind all day, I didn't let myself dwell on all that had transpired. It was weird enough that nearly every detail from the moments with Shroding stood alight in my memory as if they had happened only seconds ago instead of hours; I didn't need to add to it by ruminating on them. Yet the only time my mind seemed truly clear was when I thought of the supposed prince. Which was proving very hard not to do.

The sun seemed to sit unmoving in the sky, taunting me with the responsibilities I couldn't seem to keep up with. After the frost the other night, most of this harvest would spoil.

The day was not hot, but the sun was blistering to me. I slipped into the barn, deciding to spend a few hours prepping the bundles Micah would take into town later that evening.

"Haya..." Shroding's voice called in my mind. I dropped the stacks I had spent the last half hour wrapping.

Two eyes flashed in the upper corner of my vision. I whirled around, searching the rafters as the dark figure moved. My heart was instantly in my throat, and my fight or flight response was set wholly on flight.

Faint purring echoed in the dim barn.

"Iri?" I heaved a sigh, sliding down the wooden pillar behind me. I slumped on the ground, waiting for my heartbeat to normalize. "What the heck is wrong with me?" I looked around the barn once more, searching for familiar cat eyes, but was greeted by darkness.

"Came to startle me and leave?" I asked the air. "Typical cat."

I was sure I'd heard Shroding's voice in my head, but there was no way he could speak to me while I was awake. At least, it didn't seem possible... He was in a pocket dimension; just as he'd said, our worlds should not be able to touch. Unless he *was* in my world somehow.

I got to my feet, brushing off my pants. There was only one way to get these thoughts out of my system. I needed to validate the truth of the prophecy Shroding had spoken of.

Though I did not know the best way to start, a good place to look would be the old stone library in town. The only problem was that meant leaving the farm. The last thing my mother wanted me to do.

The farm needed all the attention I could afford, but maybe a few hours... No. A promise is a promise, and I'd said I wouldn't leave.

I hurried out of the barn; the day had quickly turned to dusk. I suppose I had outlasted the dogged sun by loading up the wagon all afternoon.

Hooves clipped down the path, dirt clouding gently behind them as Etienne and Micah drew closer. The lights flickered inside the house, indicating the kids were already inside washing up to head home.

"I got it from here, Haya," Micah said, hopping off Etienne.

I tried not to focus too much on his calling me Haya instead of Haybale. Though I hated the nickname, I hated it less when he said it.

"How is Misha doing?" I asked, as I had not seen him since he had spent the night and left early the next day.

"Better, just in time for her birthday."

"Wow, it's already that late in the season?" I mused.

"Mhm," he replied, walking off to the barn. I followed after him.

"I already loaded up the wagon with the orders," I offered dutifully, hoping for him to show some kind of appreciation for my efforts.

"I see that," was all he said as he hooked up Etienne to pull the load out of the barn. I hurried over to help strap the other side, giving it a good tug to be sure the bundles were extra secure.

"Do you need me to stay again tonight? I can come back after dropping off the kids," Micah offered, coming around to my side of the wagon.

My brows knit together. I could not help noting his choice of saying "need" instead of "want." He would stay if I needed him to but not if I wanted him to? Was I really just an obligation to him? Were we not even friends anymore?

"No, I'll be okay."

He looked unconvinced.

"Really," I promised, and knotted the rope one more time. "There," I breathed, satisfied with my work.

He laid his hand on top of mine.

"Like I told you before, it's okay to need people."

"What if I don't want to need you?" I looked up at him, searching his chestnut eyes. "What if I just wanted to want you, would that be enough?" I glared, provoked by his concerned gaze. He could stare concerned at me all day, but I didn't want his worry. I wanted his heart, his passion.

He looked serious for a few moments. I watched the light of the waning sun cast yellow and orange shadows over his face. He stepped forward, his hand tightening over mine as he angled himself in front of me. The other lifted to cup the back of my neck. It was sweaty from the hours in the barn, but he didn't seem to notice.

I braced myself, leaning heavily on the edge of the wagon. My whole body tensed like it did when I used to pretend sword fight with Theo and he went in for the killing blow.

Micah's face was inches from mine.

I couldn't breathe. I should want this, I had practically asked for it, but I wasn't sure that I did. A flash of another kiss played through my mind.

Etienne whinnied in fear and jerked the wagon, causing us both to stumble, our hands ripping off of the side of the wagon.

Micah caught me around the waist as I stumbled.

"What the..." He trailed off, the moment we shared quickly forgotten, as he looked at the retreating wagon. "I have to..." He shifted, letting me go and jogging over to Etienne, who was stomping his hooves, clearly upset.

I walked back to the porch, dumbfounded. Why had I panicked? I had been waiting years for that kiss.

Out of the corner of my eye, I thought I saw a fox-like tail disappear into the stalks.

The porch door clanged shut. I jumped, startled.

"Night, Haya," Olivia said as she hugged my legs.

I had completely forgotten about the kids.

"Night." I smiled. "Uh, did you see..." I trailed off, thinking it better to forget the almost kiss.

"Yeah, you and Micah kissing." She giggled. I opened my mouth to correct her. "Mean kitty scared Eti." She furrowed her brow and tilted her head like she was an adult disapproving of a child. I almost laughed.

"Hurry on home, okay?" I nudged her.

She and the others hurried to where Micah stood, having calmed Etienne some.

A wave of dismay made me jittery as Micah walked over to me. If I got close to him again, something might actually happen. A part of me would not have minded, in fact would have welcomed it now that I was more prepared, but a whole other part of me was more convinced than ever that Micah had only proposed out of commitment to my family and not out of love for me.

I hurried up the porch stairs and waved goodbye as I

opened the screen door. He stopped his approach, but in the scant light I couldn't see his face.

"Good night, Micah," I called, grinning brightly, hoping to mask my awkwardness.

He lifted his hand, and I slipped into the house.

I leaned against the door, taking deep breaths until I heard the wagons pull away. I locked the doors and windows, checking everything twice before eating and washing up for the day.

Before my head hit the pillow, I saw Iri sitting on the sill outside my second-story window, the shadow of the dormer covering his body. Did he want to be let inside? I was just about to get up and let him in when I heard the front door open and promptly close.

A jolt of fear had my teeth on edge as I sat up in bed.

"Who is it?" I wondered, scrambling out of bed. My heart raced with alarm as I tried to think who could possibly be coming though our front door at such a late hour. Only my family had a key to get in. It had to be my family, then. It was the only reasonable conclusion.

They had finally come home.

CHAPTER 13

You'd Get Your Knuckles Bloody For Me

The thud of footsteps on the stairs startled me from my paralyzed position. I threw open my door to see Micah standing in the hall looking chagrined.

"Oh Strings! Haya, I didn't think you would still be awake."

"Micah." My face fell.

He smiled, but it did not reach his eyes. My expectation must've been obvious.

He knew I'd expected my family.

"Sorry."

"No, it's okay..." I shivered as the cold from the hall crept into my room. "I guess you have a key to the house?"

Micah reached into his back pocket, pulling out the brass piece. "Theo gave it to me when he left. Wanted me to check in on you from time to time."

"Imagine that." I shrugged sarcastically. "What are you doing here?"

He gave an embarrassed grunt and turned around,

pulling on the rope to the attic. "Do you remember what your dad gave you for your eighth birthday?"

"Yes. He made me a dollhouse."

"Well, I was wondering if you could part with it?"

I stepped out into the hall as he unfolded the ladder.

"You want to give it to Misha?"

"I haven't been able to go out and get her anything, and I don't have the time to make something as extravagant as what your dad did. She sees Armond like a father, I think it would mean a lot to her. That is if you are okay letting it go?" He looked uncomfortable, like it pained him to make such a simple request.

I saw Misha as family, so it was an easy thing to agree to.

"Of course, Micah." My heart softened. "It's not even a question."

"This really means a lot to me too," he whispered, turning back to me.

"Why come get it now? I mean, you seemed surprised I was awake—were you just going to take it and not ask me?"

"I was just going to bring it down and ask you in the morning."

"So you were going to stay here even though I told you I would be fine."

"We both know you are anything but fine." He tapped the side of the ladder once, then paused, twice, pause, and then a quick one-one. It was a code we used rarely, as the simple phrase "I'm here" represented a dependency, a trust far greater than the words could convey.

I touched his elbow, moving to stand alongside him in the dark hall.

As much as I wanted to ignore our almost kiss earlier, I

could not stop myself from needing an answer. Was he in love with me or not?

"Micah." I lifted my chin, hardening my resolve. "Do you love me?"

His golden hair fell around his face as he turned, taking my hand in his.

"How can you even ask that? Of course I do."

He leaned back on the ladder rungs, pulling me in front of him. In the dark hall I could not make out his expression.

"I-I—" How did I tell him that I didn't believe him, that I doubted his love?

"Haybale." He wrapped his hand around my long braid, rolling it around his arm. "We ground each other. We are good for each other. Where is this doubt coming from?" He lifted his head.

"Am I just a responsibility to you?" I stepped closer, drawn in by my hair wrapped around his arm.

"If that were all, would I do this?" His free hand gripped the fabric of my nightgown at the small of my back and roughly pulled me against his chest.

I gasped as sparks of pleasure rippled across my skin.

"Kiss me," I begged.

"I did not come here for this." Micah exhaled, his voice low and sounding much as it had the night on the lounge.

"My heart is yours, has been for years," I offered, needing the truth of my feelings to be known.

I gasped as his lips closed over mine.

He tasted of bonfire and a snowy mountain breeze. It was everything my fourteen-year-old self had dreamed it would be, and yet it was nothing like when I'd kissed Shroding.

"By the Strings," I cried, wrenching out of Micah's grasp. Heat flooded my face. I had kissed the Prince of Shamar. I looked up at Micah, who blinked, genuinely confused. I never swore. I was completely messing everything up.

"Was it that good, or that bad?" Micah raised an eyebrow, but I could tell from the way he scratched his left bicep that he was nervous.

Micah, my longtime crush, had just kissed me. Why was I thinking about the prince?

"It's really late. I just freaked out a little."

"Haya, I would never do anything you didn't want me to."

I smiled. Of course I knew that, Micah would always protect me. The thought both gave me peace and made me sad.

"I should go get that dollhouse, you'll never find it up there." I nodded and brushed past him to climb up the rungs. "Wait down here, okay? I just need a minute."

He nodded, understanding me better than most. He would give me space to figure out how I was feeling.

I climbed up into the small cavity, coughing as I pushed through the cobwebs. Our attic was like most, dusty and full of trivial keepsakes and unnecessary clutter. Mother and Father had always talked about cleaning it out, but they never got around to it.

The moonlight shone through a small circular window across from me, casting light on the droppings from some little critters. I shivered, unenthused with the idea that things were living up here. I could only hope none of them were bats. I could handle a few squirrels but not bats. I eased past some boxes and shuffled some old decor. I was pretty sure I knew what box my old dollhouse was in. I shuffled around, careful of the boxes labeled dishware. Dust was heavy in the air, and I sneezed as a puff burst into my face.

"They should have cleaned this place out in the last seventeen years," I complained, sliding another few boxes out of the way, clearing a path. I was deep into the attic, the light barely reaching me in the corner of the cramped room. I tripped over something that sounded like bells rattling at my feet. *Creepy.* I shuddered and inched closer to the box in the corner labeled Haya's Toys. "There you are." I moved with purpose, quickly, stepping over boxes and bins on the floor. I jumped when I kicked a support beam with my foot and the wall beside me rattled. Startled by the vibration, a swarm of bats flew out of the shadows. I screamed and backed into the wall, falling on my butt as my foot sank into one of the floorboards. The bats flew around until they escaped through whatever opening they had come in by. I grasped my heart as I sat on the floor trying to steady my breath. "I said anything but bats," I wheezed to no one in particular.

Once calm, I looked at the board that had caught my foot. It moved up and down like a seesaw. I pulled it back as far as it would go and saw a worn yellow book wedged in the small space. I reached down and pulled it out. It had no title, publisher or author. The cover was a soft but thick yellow leather. I had never seen this book before. I turned it around in my hands, flipping through the pages. They were all flimsy and some blackened and scorched. Carefully I tucked it under my arm, righting the broken floorboard. Standing, I dusted off my dress and looked for my box of toys. The box was only a few more paces away. I moved carefully, wary of more wobbly floorboards. The box was old but in good condition. I awkwardly tried to lift it and failed. The box was too big to carry while holding the yellow book.

"Drop something on your foot?" Micah teased, calling up

the ladder. "I heard you scream?" The rungs of the ladder squeaked as if he was climbing up.

"I'm fine, thanks for asking." I rolled my eyes. "Coming down now." I placed the book on a bin next to me and lifted the dollhouse. The way out seemed much easier than the way in, even with the large box in my hands. I met Micah by the ladder, and we carried the house down together.

"This is bigger than I thought it would be."

Sweat dotted my forehead. "A lot heavier too." Micah smiled his easy grin, all strangeness from the kiss before forgotten. "Yeah, I guess some things don't get smaller as we get bigger."

"Guess so. I think Misha will love it, though, don't you?"

"Definitely," I agreed.

Micah took the box and moved to take it downstairs. I touched his arm, halting him.

"Micah, it's pretty late. Why don't you stay the night and ride back in the morning. Less of a chance Misha will discover her present," I teased, hoping it was not as suggestive as it sounded.

He placed the box on the floor, replacing me in his arms. Brushing my hair over my shoulder, he leaned in and kissed me again.

His lips were soft, familiar in a way I didn't think kissing someone only twice should feel.

Maybe I was just doing it wrong.

I forced my eyes closed as Micah moved me back against the frame of my bedroom door.

His hands were at my hips, lifting and holding me up against the wall. Micah had always been bulky, but I had never felt so small with him before. My toes brushed the floor as I tried to find traction, the movement bunching up my nightgown in the process.

The chill of the hall brushed across exposed skin, a harsh contrast to the heat of his hands.

It all was so new, so good. We should stop. Why did I want him to stop?

His hands found the hem of my gown, which had rolled up to my midthigh. When he palmed my bare leg, I nearly jumped out of my skin.

He moaned, and the sound triggered a stomach-dropping wave of panic that ripped through my core. This was all happening too fast. I wasn't even close to being prepared for this. How had we gotten here? We had never even gone on a date before.

A growl, low and wild, had us both freezing with fear.

CHAPTER 14

Golden Hair, Pale Gray Eyes

Iridescent eyes flashed in the unlit hall. Iri's large form moved from the shadows. He crouched low, teeth bared, flint eyes fixated on Micah.

"Hey, no, it's alright," I cooed, taking Micah's moment of surprise to extricate myself. I dropped to the floor in front of Iri. "Calm down." I ran my fingers through his fur, gently soothing him. "How did you even get inside?" I murmured.

"When did you start letting strays into the house?" Micah's tone was clearly disapproving, and I frowned up at him.

Iri bared his teeth once more, a low warning in his chest. I scratched him behind his black-tipped ears, using everything I knew about cats to try and calm him.

I was defensive, and even though I too was annoyed and confused by Iri's sudden appearance, I was unusually protective of him as well.

"He is persistent and acts more like a guard dog than a cat. But what does it matter? He's not going to hurt you," I snapped, doing my best to quell the bubbling consternation in my body. I was only half-certain Iri wouldn't hurt anyone. He was a wild cat, after all.

"It's just odd." Micah tilted his head. "I didn't mean to upset you. I was just surprised."

Iri had stopped growling and nudged his way past us and into my room.

I stood, shifting awkwardly in the hallway. "See, it's all fine, he was probably just as surprised as we were."

"Yeah, right." Micah brushed his sandy hair away from his eyes. "We should sleep," he relented, turning and disappearing into Theo's room. Timeworn springs squeaked in the dark.

I waited for a beat, debating following him.

"Micah?" I tapped on the ajar door.

He sat on the bed inspecting the photos of him and my brother decorating the back wall.

"Theo would have killed me for"—he gestured vaguely to the hallway—"taking advantage like that." He pulled one of the pictures down, cradling it in his hands before placing it on the bed next to him. It was of us as kids the summer Micah moved to Wycliff from Romath. Theo was missing his front teeth, knocked out when Micah and he had roughhoused earlier that day. My arms were wrapped happily around Micah's neck. "I know we haven't heard anything. I know now there is little hope. But..." His voice caught. "I check the mailbox every day... in the hopes that news will come." The anguish in his voice brought tears I thought I had finished shedding to my eyes. "It feels like I've failed him. Like I keep failing him."

"Like you told me, it was his choice to leave, to enlist

when he did. Besides, we don't know anything yet," I said with a confidence I didn't feel.

"Haya, I..." he started, and shook his head. "I'm pretty tired." He moved the picture to the desk, placing it facedown.

"Right, of course," I said, turning to leave.

"Let me know if you have any nightmares, okay?"

I nodded, then paused. Micah's family was originally from the capital, and his father, Mr. Ilsan, had worked in a high-ranked position in the military. Perhaps there was a chance that maybe Micah knew more about the prince than he let on. He had been so interested in the change to the school history book, and though talking about his dad was a touchy subject, I had to at least try to find out if what Shroding had said was remotely accurate.

"Micah, did your dad ever tell you about his work?"

"Occasionally."

I stroked the end of my braid, thinking through the few things Shroding had shared with me. It was unlikely that Mr. Ilsan had any knowledge of a prince, but perhaps he knew about the creatures attacking me—Wraiths, Shroding had called them.

"Did he tell you anything about soldiers with vibration sickness?" I glanced at him.

Micah's brow furrowed. "The Grieving? We both know they are half-alive soldiers crippled by using their vibration gift on themselves."

"Have you ever heard about them becoming shadows when they die?"

Micah's eyes narrowed in the dark room. Neither of us reached for the light, as if saying these things warranted the darkness. "You heard about that? It's not common knowledge."

So it was true, then. What Shroding had said about the Wraiths being those who died from the sickness. "Do the... shadows have a name?"

I could not see Micah's expression clearly, but I could make out the way his hands fisted the coverlet of the bed. "Wraiths, they are called Wraiths."

"Did your father tell you anything else about the..." I swallowed hard, "Wraiths?"

"They have the power to possess humans." He paused. "Haya, why are you asking me this, did you read something?"

"Is there anything else you can tell me?" I pressed, needing more proof, more certainty.

"He used to say, you will know someone has been possessed when their eyes glow purple," he offered.

"Do you think they are real?" I asked, my voice a whisper as I wanted so badly for him to deny it, to tell me they were not real, because I would believe him over some lost prince. I would believe my childhood friend over anyone else right now. I wanted so badly for all of it to be a nightmare and nothing more.

He rose from the bed. "They were real to my father," he affirmed, which meant they were real to him. He came towards me, his steps loud in the stillness of the room. When his hand reached up to my cheek, it was cold, as if all the warmth had left his body. I shivered. "Haya, how do you know about the Wraiths?"

My throat was dry. Shroding had been right. If they were real and they were after me, then I really was not safe. "Just something Father told me once." I pulled his hand from my cheek, giving it a squeeze. "It's just morbid curiosity, nothing more," I assured him, making my voice light and uninterested.

"Haya... let's talk more about this tomorrow, okay?"

"Okay," I agreed, grateful he didn't press to talk more about it tonight. I turned to leave. "Goodnight, Mic—"

"I'm sorry if I took things too far... before," he cut in, making me pause in my retreat. He dropped his head, flaxen hair falling over his eyes in an obvious attempt to hide his shamed expression.

"We both got carried away," I hedged.

We had touched and kissed more in the last day than we ever had in the last seven years we had been friends. I didn't know if that meant he liked me or just liked kissing me. Regardless, my ego was lifted by the attention; at least Micah seemed to like my kisses, where Shroding most definitely had not.

He smiled his easy grin, and I found it just as comforting as it had always been. Maybe things wouldn't be as awkward as I'd thought.

"Before we take things any further, I ought to take you on a real date." He stepped closer, taking my hand in his and lifting it to his lips for a soft kiss. "What do you say, want to go out with your future husband?"

"Oh?" I blinked, the awkwardness I had hoped to avoid rearing its unnerving head. Butterflies bounced in my stomach. Husband? I hadn't agreed to his proposal, had I? All we had done was kiss, and yet people got wed for less. Perhaps a date was just what I needed to make a decision. A date would mean going to town, which also meant I could go to the library, a great opportunity to get answers in regards to a certain prince. "I was actually hoping to go into town," I agreed heartily.

"I was thinking I could set something up here for you," he offered.

"Oh, well, yes... you could." I deflated, hoping my despondent demeanor might warrant some doting, as it always had with my father. "Honestly," I sighed, forlorn, "I need to get off the farm for a while. I'm kinda losing my mind here." It wasn't a lie, I did need to get out. I needed to figure out what was going on for sure, but I also just needed to get away from wheat, work and the anxiety that had not left my bones since my family left.

Micah softened, nodding with understanding. "I get what you mean. Truly." He reached out to hug me, and I let him. It was safe, easy being with him, like nothing had changed when so many things had. "We can go out tomorrow," he caved, pulling away with a mischievous smile. "I know just the thing."

He was up to something, and in truth I didn't need another mystery to solve. Still, I had no reason not to trust Micah.

"Then it's a date," I agreed.

"Goodnight, Haybale." He tapped the coded phrase into the wood frame next to us.

"Goodnight, Micah," I whispered, walking through and closing the door to my room.

I breathed in, resting my head against the door. I turned on the light, trying to chase away the shadows of the conversation with Micah. Soft purring met my ears, and I looked across the room at Iri.

He sat carefully on the window seat, his dark eyes unblinking.

"Iri," I scolded. "That was not okay, scaring us like that."

He dropped his head to the sill, a deep sigh puffing out his stomach and sweeping the scraps of paper I'd left on the bench, from the day Theo had left, to the floor.

I frowned, walking over to clean up the mess.

Lifting the scraps, I collected them in my palm. I should probably throw them away. One white paper began to unfold, and I noticed the etching of a word.

"Heed."

It was in Theo's haphazard hand.

I carried the folded papers to my desk, laying them out and unfurling one after another, till the message was complete.

"Should I fall, heed his call. Trust where I did not," I read aloud.

Iri lifted his head, moving to sit next to where I stood.

I repeated the words again.

Was this a joke? A mistake, another game of Theo's?

"What do you think it means?" I asked my furry friend.

Iri's ears twitched. Purring, he trotted to my bed and curled up over top the patterned stars.

"You're right, maybe it will make more sense in the morning."

Confused and weary, I crawled into bed, letting much-needed rest take me.

I woke in a black space. Darkness billowed around me like a falling curtain. I floated weightless, a yellow leather book in my hand. I opened it, the pages burnt and crumbling. I looked around uncertainly at the nothingness that surrounded me.

An invisible hand gripping my gown jerking me forward through the dark. I thought to scream, but I did not feel fear like I had in other dreams. The hand dragged me till I stood facing a warm fireplace. The room was feathered and unclear, but I could make out a tall bookshelf and red chaise to my right.

The book slipped from my hands and floated up to the bookshelf before me. The shelves were filled with yellow books wedged together, save for a single gap which the book in my hand slid into. I backed away from the shelf. Something in this dream didn't feel right. A face, one I had never seen before, flickered before my eyes. Golden hair, pale gray eyes. He was handsome like Shroding, but his edges seemed harder, almost threadbare. He reached for me, and I turned to run from the room.

I was moving slowly, like my body was outside the speed of the dream. The room flipped over onto itself and melted like candle wax, changing into a new room with white tiled walls and marble floors. I was in a bathroom. An oversized claw-foot tub stood before me. I stepped forward to see a cat at the bottom. I reached for the cat, but the basin was much deeper than it had appeared from afar, and the cat was too far below, nothing but a speck against the smooth white porcelain. The animal cried out in pain. I reached down, trying to help the cat. It looked so familiar, but in the dream, I could not place it. The tub filled with water, and the cat struggled to swim, sinking to the bottom. I felt panick and terror for the animal. But my terror soon was directed at my own safety. I grabbed my throat, gasping to breathe, as if I too was in the tub drowning.

The dream flashed a bright white, and a dark-haired boy lay in the tub, blood turning the water red around him. I could not see where he was bleeding, but he was unconscious in the red pool. I reached out to him but was pulled back by an invisible hand.

I screamed, calling to him and thrashing uselessly against the force. I had to help him! I had to save him!

The world spun until I was holding the yellow book again,

the leather feeling like sandpaper against my hands. I was falling into the blackness as his name repeated in my mind. Shroding. Shroding. Shroding.

The boy I could not reach.

The boy I needed to save.

CHAPTER 15

The Moon Holds The Hidden Crown

I pulled myself from the dream in what seemed like stages. First I was scared, then pained, lastly gripped with urgency. I sat up with an alertness I hadn't had for weeks. The yellow journal in the dream looked the same as the one in the attic, the one I had completely forgotten about in all the excitement last night.

The sun had not yet begun to rise. Still, I got out of bed, rebraiding my hair and cinching it with my favorite leather cord. Feeling like I had a clue, I bolted from my room and drew the folding ladder down. My heart raced with expectation and dread. There was no way the books could be related. I'd just dreamed about it because it was in my subconscious.

A large part of me wanted to come down empty-handed so I could go back to the way things were just days ago; waiting for my mom to come home with Father and Theo. I stumbled up the rungs and hesitated, only slightly worried the bats might have come back.

Poking my head through the opening, I scanned the dark space for the yellow book, the hairs on my neck standing on end. I was being watched. I wanted to shrink back, to go down the ladder and pretend the book really meant nothing. Perhaps it did. Perhaps if this had been a week ago, I would have descended the ladder and thought nothing of it, but not anymore.

I carefully shuffled to where I last saw the book. It lay on the box from the other day, exactly where I had left it. I picked it up and made my way back to my room. Everything in me wanted to run, but I forced myself to move slowly so I didn't fall like last time or startle whatever was watching me, whether bats or something else. I tried not to think of what that something else might be. Once in the hall I latched the ladder back into place on the ceiling.

Iri sat in my doorway, eyes on the yellow book.

I shuffled past him and sat on my bed, looking accusingly at the yellow book. It was old, the binding ripping, and the few intact pages were trimmed with gold. I flipped it over in my lap. It was soft, unlike the sandpaper I had experienced in my dream. I opened it, the pages sticking together. I carefully turned each page. A scribble of lines, words I did not under-stand blanketed the page, leaving no margins, just edge-to-edge ink in a language I had never seen before. I flipped a few more pages, looking for anything I could actually read.

It wasn't till I got to the last few pages that the words became legible. They did not say much, but what they did caused my heart to race and nearly stop.

The power of the king unleashed
The redemption of the world made complete
Though shadows of death are released
Call for aid and do not retreat

The moon holds the hidden crown,
An amethyst shine on silver discerns
What is needed shall be passed down
Until the prince returns

The book slipped through my fingers, though I did not acknowledge when it fell to the floor with a *thud*.

I rubbed my fingertips together, and they were rough like sandpaper.

I shivered and looked up. Iri.

He had not moved from the doorway, his gold-flecked black eyes vigilant; waiting.

I had been hopeful that things might go back to normal, but I did not think that would ever be possible. Even if I had not found the journal, Iri, the unusual but beautiful cat, would still mean something. His showing up that day on the dandelion hill, his attention, his watchfulness was somehow connected to Shroding. Though I was not sure how.

I placed the yellow book on the corner of my nightstand. I had so many questions and no real answers, at least none I was sure of, or wanted to believe. More than anything I just wanted it all to go away. I turned and strode over to the door, kneeling to push Iri out my open bedroom door. He didn't budge. It was like pushing a solid stone wall.

"Go away," I protested. "I don't need a cat gargoyle to keep monsters away."

I was too annoyed to laugh, but the irony of how much I really did need someone to keep the monsters away—just an unearthly attractive prince, not a weird cat—was not lost on me.

Iri purred louder and looked at me, almost smiling with his eyes as if catching the irony as well.

Ignoring my clamoring, he bounded effortlessly past me to my bed, curling up once more on the etched stars.

"Cats," I grumbled, "give them an inch."

I closed my bedroom door sighing.

"You know, you don't look fat, but you seem pretty heavy."

His eyes opened, and he looked almost wary of me, as if nervous I would try to pick him up.

"I won't pick you up, you bizarre beast," I fussed sardonically.

His ears twitched.

"Haya." The sound of my name filled my mind, and a wash of shock and joy pounded my heart. It was Shroding, his voice in my head again. For a second, I thought it was somehow the cat but quickly dismissed that thought. I leaned unsteadily against the door for a moment, letting the sound melt into my memory, trying hard to keep my thoughts at bay. Just as quickly as the sound had come, it was gone, and my uninhibited thoughts flooded in. I walked over to the bed and sat down, putting my head in my hands, and groaned.

"I'm seriously losing it." I flopped back on the bed, careful not to hit Iri with my legs. I reached over and turned out the light I had left on after the conversation with Micah. The room was unnervingly dark without the lamp or even the moonlight to chase away shadows. I reached over to switch it back on but hesitated. Taking a deep breath, I lay back down and waited for my eyes to adjust.

"Can I tell you something crazy?" I said to the night and the purring cat at my feet. As annoyed as I was, his presence was still comforting. He did not answer, of course, but instead I felt him stand and walk over to my side, flopping down next to my waist, his purr vibrating at my hip.

I reached down till my hand found his velvety ears. I gently stroked his fur. "This is not going to become a regular thing," I promised him, even though it had pretty much already become a nightly occurrence.

He yawned in response, undeterred by my order.

"I've been having nightmares for a while now," I whispered. "Terrible creatures killing me, the farm destroyed and then a prince." I chuckled darkly. "A very uncomfortably attractive prince," I mumbled to myself. The purring seemed to hiccup for a second and then continue. "I don't know why, but I believe him. That he's really a prince, the lost prince," I said softly, thinking about the poem. "Though shadows of death are released, call for aid and do not retreat." Could the shadows be referencing the Wraiths? Shroding had told me to call for him and he would keep me safe from them. Where had the journal come from and why was it hiding in a floorboard in the attic? Theo's note churned in my mind. *Heed his call, trust where I did not?* Was the call somehow connected to Shroding as well? It was all so confusing, and how did Iri fit into it? "I think you're involved. I think you are connected to the prince." I put my hands to my face. "Strings, it sounds absurd saying it aloud."

"Haya." Shroding's voice entered my mind again, making me gasp.

"By the Strings!" I cried, covering my ears and rolling over, my face pressed into the pillow. I had officially lost it. Talking to a mysterious cat that couldn't stop purring, and hearing voices of a dead, or lost, prince—maybe the trauma and stress of losing my family and running the farm was finally breaking me.

Iri's eyes remained closed, uninterested in my outburst.

Aggravated at myself, I rolled over, clutching my pillow

tightly to my chest. I closed my eyes and listened to the silver cat begin to groom himself dutifully. I listened to the rhythmic strokes, a soothing quality to the sound, as it mixed with his soft purring. The tension faded from my shoulders as Iri methodically lulled me into sleep.

CHAPTER 16

Who Are You?

The king's crest was the first thing I saw etched into the floor in gold.

Then the rest of the room came into view. The arching ceiling rose high; a beautiful mural covered it and poured down the walls, images of Shamar under a twilight sky. Each major city was represented on the walls of the grand room. The marble floor led up to a circular platform at the far end of the space.

Slowly I walked to the platform, stopping at the ascending stairs. The room was dimly lit, the only light coming from the glass dome over the platform. The light filtered in, illuminating a jeweled throne. At its base, light reflected off a four-winged creature made of gold, which held up the seat. The creature was the symbol of the king. Though I had never been there before—I knew this was the throne room in Castle Judahall in the capital city of Romath.

The thumps of someone walking around downstairs woke me. For a few heartbeats, I lay perfectly still, recalling the great room till the deep rumble of purring along my hip drew my attention. Iri lay lazy against my side, his eyes closed in wavy slits. His tiny lashes gave him a cuteness his large muscular form did not normally give off. For a moment he seemed sweet, like a fluffy stuffed animal I could bury my face in.

"Haybale?" Micah called, opening the door to my room.

Iri's eyes popped open, nose sniffing the air.

"Morning, Micah." I smiled, sitting up in bed, my cheeks warming. "What's this?" I asked, eyeing the tray he carried in.

Micah smiled at me, about to speak, but stopped when he saw Iri.

He set the tray down in front of me. It was full of fruits and scones from the bakery in town. My mouth salivated. Micah walked over to my window and pulled the curtain back, revealing the afternoon sun. Where had the day gone?

"I thought you would enjoy the fruits of all your labor. Your favorite scones. I realized yesterday, preparing to celebrate Misha's birthday, that I never got the chance to celebrate yours over the summer. With your father and brother leaving and all the extra work on the farm, it kept getting put off." He turned around, his easy grin wide across his face. "So tonight I'm going to take you out as promised. You always said when you were of age you wanted to go dancing at Jubilee."

"You want to take me to the club?" I laughed, finding it hard to imagine Micah in a club.

Jubilee was the one place in Wycliff that was almost up to par, or so I heard, with the clubs in Erasmus, which had all the latest advancements money could buy. Most of the soldiers stationed at the Citadel went there to blow off steam, but it was not cheap or easy to get into.

"It will make for a very memorable first date." He laughed.

I popped the buttery moist scone into my mouth. "Icantimagine"—I swallowed, clearing my throat—"you dancing?" In all the years I had known Micah, I had never seen him dance once.

"Yeah, I'm not sure how fun it will be," he warned, his signature smile spreading over his tanned face, "but I remember it's what you said you wanted to do for your seventeenth."

My heart was so full.

"How long have you been planning this?" I smirked, knowing getting access to the club was over a week's wait. Also Micah would not have been able to plan a trip to town to get my favorite scones for a breakfast-in-bed surprise all in one short night.

He shifted, his cheeks turning pink. "Well, yeah, I needed to get some things ready."

My cheeks hurt from how wide I was smiling. I tilted my head and raised an eyebrow. "What things?" I coyly gestured to the plate before me. "This?"

"Yes, that"—he rubbed his flaxen hair shyly—"and I took care of the kids and the farm already, so you don't have to do any work today. I made a reservation for dinner after dancing. I figure we will work up an appetite."

My eyes went wide at how thought-out the plan was. I turned to Iri, who watched me with his dark gaze.

I pinched both of his ears, wiggling them excitedly.

"Did you hear that I'm off duty today!" I laughed, weightless.

Micah chuckled as well. "All I want you to do is relax and get ready. Okay?"

I beamed. Iri was less impressed, swatting my hands away with his large paw. He rose from the bed and padded swiftly out of my room.

"Yes, it sounds wonderful, when do we leave?"

———

My excitement lessened exponentially as evening approached. I had spent the last few hours getting ready as requested but only got more stressed as time passed. Micah had already mailed my letter to Talie and brought the books back to the library as I had left them out on the kitchen counter. I knew Micah was just trying to be nice, to lift my spirits. He was putting in a lot of effort to do so, but that only made it worse. My reasons for going to town were not as pure as his. Having fun, going dancing, relishing a stress-free night were not my objectives. To him this was the beginning of our relationship, but for me this was... what? A wild goose chase? No, Shroding was real, and the journal was proof that a prince existed. I just needed to figure out how to find him. How to set him free. I intended to learn more about my night-mares and the Wraiths. It was time I stopped running from the nightmares and faced whatever was happening to me. I had fallen asleep twice but had not moved dimensions as Shroding had said. So how was I supposed to face what was happening, how was I to help him if I couldn't talk to him?

I dressed in the only fancy outfit I owned, a flowy lace dress my mom had gotten me for my seventeenth birthday. She had teased me, saying I would wear it on a date with Micah. The joke seemed like a lifetime ago, and its accuracy almost made me refrain from wearing it. I borrowed a pair of practical heels from my mom's closet and a long tan peacoat that was better suited for a night out than my puffy fur-lined green one, which I was sure smelled of farm.

I picked up the yellow journal from my desk and tucked it into the inside pocket of my coat. It was small enough not to be noticed under the fabric. I twisted my hair up, leaving a few pieces out around my face. It would have to do; other than a braid, I wasn't skilled at doing my own hair.

The sun danced low on the horizon as if wanting to linger and join in the fun at Jubilee.

I met Micah on the steps outside.

He waited next to Etienne, his light hair styled back, a gray coat covering black pants and a plain vest top. He was so basic even when he tried to dress up. It was endearing.

"Your chariot awaits, my lady..." Micah said, arms out, gesturing to Etienne. His gaze traveled over my outfit, and my cheeks flushed.

"I wasn't really sure what one should wear dancing..." I pulled the coat around my body. A dress might have been a bad idea, I forgot I would be riding a horse to town. I had not ridden sidesaddle in many years.

"You're perfect," he praised me.

I walked over, looking nervously at Etienne's back.

"Whoa," I gasped as Micah lifted me effortlessly by the waist and deposited me in the saddle. I grab the horn to keep from falling.

"I'll lock up, sit tight." Micah hurried up the porch, the sconces flickering in the cold night.

I looked towards the gate, where something scintillated for a moment in the growing moonlight. I squinted to make out the figure, chills running up my spine. The shape was shadowed by the trees, but I knew what it was.

Iri.

He sat at the gate, his dark eyes reflecting the porch light. Did the cat expect to follow me to town as well? I could feel Iri's judgy gaze as Micah climbed up behind me, draping a blanket over my shoulders. I half expected Iri to jump in front of Etienne, scaring him again.

"Ready?" Micah asked, his low question rumbling against my back. His lips caressed the shell of my ear, and I nearly slipped from the saddle.

Micah wrapped his arms around my waist, pressing me back into him. I swallowed thickly and opened my mouth to respond.

"Don't go." Shroding's voice was soft, pleading. I looked back at the gate and felt the same unease as last night. I only heard Shroding's voice when Iri was around. The connection was not lost on me. It was almost as if Shoding and Iri were one and the same. The apocalypse of that thought rocked me to the core, and like last night, I tried to reason it to be impossible. Because it was impossible—not even the vibration gift could transform people.

I shook my head, trying to shake loose his voice and the thoughts it dredged up. For a moment, I almost decided not to go. I almost backed out. For a moment I got a sinking feeling that something about this outing was going to go terribly wrong.

I closed my eyes. *Shroding.* I thought as hard as I could to send this message to wherever he was. *I will get answers. I will find out the truth, and when I do, you better be ready.* When I opened my eyes Iri was gone, but Shroding's response filled my mind.

"I will be."

CHAPTER 17

A Date To Die For

The ride was quiet, the chill of the night making me grateful for Micah's forethought with the blanket. We rode into town, the dirt road turning to gravel, making us bounce for a while till it leveled out into smooth stone slabs.

"They started decorating today for the Celebration of Strings," Micah said, pointing to the lights hanging between lamp posts.

"Already?" I asked, turning my face so I could see him.

"It is in a few weeks, they do it around this time every year." Micah looked at me, confused.

"Sorry, I guess I forgot it was so soon, with the farm and everything..." I hadn't realized how quickly time had flown by. In all of the craziness, I had forgotten about the Celebration. A holiday to celebrate the beginning of creation. King Roark began it one hundred years into his reign. So for over four thousand years, every winter people gave presents that contained some kind of string to family and friends as a symbol of what the Creator did in the beginning.

The Creator spoke, and the sound vibrated like a string, flowing through space and time, expanding out forever. We were all tied to that beginning sound through our own vibrations. This was why those with the gift were so special. It was a manifestation of their Nephesh linked back to the Creator's voice.

"Do you still play that cello your parents got you as a gift when you were ten?" Micah asked, twisting a loose thread on the reins.

"I'm surprised you remember that." I smiled, recalling the beautiful stringed instrument.

"How can I not? It was my first Celebration with you."
I blushed.

He cleared his throat. "Plus it was a design the Seraphs brought to our world. It's really special that you got one." He was right. It was the best stringed gift I had ever received. The Seraphs had brought many unique items from the other worlds, not just technology but music, art and languages. Over the last eight hundred years, people had added hanging lights to their homes and land; on trees, bushes, balconies, and porches. Some people strung up paper snowflakes and dried fruit as a way to celebrate the Creator of Strings.

Even though the Celebration is over four thousand years old, it is still respected and acclaimed all across the land. Everyone joins in, young and old. It may be in winter, but it's the warmest time of the year. Most people hand-make something to give at the Celebration table, a meal with your whole family, extended and beyond. It was tradition for everyone to travel to one of the major cities, the celebrations lasting almost a week. There were stories about King Roark holding a party at Castle Judahall, but that was long before my time, and the steward never held parties, or so I'd heard. In fact, my family never left Wycliff for the Celebration, like the other families did. My father always said it was because we had no extended family and a duty to the farm.

We tied Etienne up in a park down the street from the club and made our way inside the storefront, a liquor shop, which was very convenient and lucrative, though not very aesthetically pleasing. The club was housed in the remodeled cellar just below the store. It was a clever way to keep anyone underage from getting access to the club.

Since those with the gift were expected to go to war at eighteen, they were given some freedom at seventeen. Bars and clubs were allowed to be patronized by anyone seventeen or older. This was done as a way to assess a person's maturity. Get inebriated too many times before you're fighting age, and you'd gain a reputation as an idiot, unreliable and unhirable for any work. It was a fairly effective method to keep youth in line.

We walked down the dark steps to the cellar. A wall of sound slammed into us as we passed through the doors to the underground club.

"This place got an upgrade," Micah yelled over the booming music. The bass pulsed in my chest.

"Have you been here before?" I asked, straining my voice to be heard over the pounding drums.

"I went on a date here a few months ago," he yelled back. "The club has a glass dance floor now," he noted, ignoring my slack-jawed expression.

The glass floor was amazing, reflecting and sparkling under the colorful lights. Smoke filled the room, making it mysterious and exciting. Like you could meet someone truly life-changing in the mists. Of course that was highly unlikely in our town.

Micah pointed at the band playing on the stage. "We got lucky tonight—they rarely do live music." He led me around the dance floor.

Who had he gone on a date with? How had I not known about it? "When did you become a club expert?" I asked instead of what I really wanted to know.

"What?" Micah yelled back. I waved it off as he steered me through the crowds to a corner by the bar. Somehow it was quieter here. "I'm going to get a drink, want anything?" Micah asked at a more normal volume, though my ears were ringing slightly.

Though I was legal now, I wasn't a big fan of alcohol, the way it burned down my throat and sat in my stomach heavy and hot. Besides, drinking was not on the agenda tonight; I had bigger mysteries to solve than how people could drink themselves into oblivion. I lifted my foot to step closer to him, my heels sticking to the floor, making me cringe. Why had I wanted to come here at all when I was of age? Did I think this would be fun? I suppose I had, back then. Now, I wasn't so convinced.

"No, I'm okay, I think I'll just head to the dance floor," I said, my voice already hoarse from yelling. I was not a loud person, and yelling to be heard was very unnatural.

"Okay, I'll find you in a little bit." He nodded. "Don't go too far from this spot, okay?"

I nodded and started to take off my coat but quickly put it back on. The book was in my pocket, and I didn't want to just leave it. But it was hot, and the mass of bodies would only grow in number as the night continued, making it hotter. I needed to find a moment to get away and get to the library. The library would close in two hours, so I would need to think of a way to ditch Micah.

I eyed the crowd, looking for the best way to cut through to the door.

A hand on my shoulder made me jump. I was greeted by a thin guy with a crew cut and a mole on his cheek.

"Wanna dance?" He was a soldier from the Citadel, the haircut told me as much. His breath, on the other hand, told me he was very intoxicated. My stomach churned as I leaned away.

"No, thank you." I smiled politely and turned to see Micah making his way back to me.

"I've got moves that will really make you sweat." The soldier leaned in, and even in the oppressive heat I could feel his breath on my neck.

I edged away as best as I could, realizing he was probably not talking about dance moves.

"Hey, man." Micah came over, sliding his hand onto my shoulder, conveniently removing Mole Guy's hand in the process. "She has a dance partner," Micah added smoothly.

Mole Guy grunted and disappeared into the crowd.

Micah placed a glass of water in front of me as he sipped his own. "Sorry to have left you. Didn't think the hounds would descend so quickly."

"It's okay." I smiled, brushing a few baby hairs away from my face. It was so hot.

"Why aren't you dancing?"

"I didn't want to leave my coat unattended."

"I'm here now, go have fun. Let off some steam."

"You're not going to dance?"

He cracked a wide grin. "When have you ever seen me dance?"

I pouted. He had come here on a date before—had he danced then? Who had he been with?

"Have you ever danced here before?" I hedged. His grin turned to a smirk.

"Are you jealous?" He mused, a coy lift to his brow that communicated he knew exactly what I'd been thinking.

An enthusiastic dancer rammed into my back, pushing me into Micah's arms. His lips caressed my ear as he whispered.

"There will be plenty of opportunity for you to see me dance the rest of our lives. Trust me, it will be worth the wait."

My face flushed scarlet as, with Mole Guy, I did not think we were talking about the same kind of dancing.

Chest to chest, he slowly slipped his hands under my coat, peeling it off my shoulders to drape it casually over his arm. I started to protest but stopped. I could trust Micah. He would keep the book safe even if he didn't know about it.

He stepped back, appraising me. His chestnut eyes danced with all the approval I needed.

Heat burned over my cheeks and down my neck. By the Strings, it was too hot.

I nodded once and dipped into the crowd.

———

I didn't know how long I had been dancing for, but it was long enough that my hair had started to stick to the back of my neck and my legs tingled, almost numb. I had surprised myself, getting lost in the music and actually having fun. Some girls on the dance floor had let me join in their protective circle after some guy had tried to grind his hips against me. I could only hope Micah had not seen the assault. Then again, if he had, he most likely would have intervened.

In desperate need of water, I made my way back to Micah. His face was impassive. I smiled brightly as he held out my water. I drank it with the thirst of a wilted plant as the music switched to a low melodic beat.

"Haya," Micah said, his tone serious.

"Yes?" I asked, my smile faltering.

"Are you ready to go to dinner? I have something I need to talk to you about..."

I froze. The sinking feeling from earlier returned, washing away any lightheartedness dancing had given me. Did Micah want to ask about the Wraiths, or about the proposal? I was such a fool. I had gotten lost having fun, needing more than I'd realized to blow off steam, and forgot to get to the library. Was it already closed?

"Right, sure..." I nodded, taking my coat and putting it back on, though it was the last thing I wanted to do after sweating so much.

A young soldier approached us, huffing and puffing.

"Thanes?" Micah asked, surprised.

Thanes was Micah's friend from the Citadel; he looked after Mrs. Ilsan, who worked there as a cook. I had never met him before. He glanced at me, his expression confused for a moment, then shook his head and focused his attention on Micah. "Man, I wish we had phone lines like in the cities..." He gasped, trying to catch his breath. "At least you told me where you would be tonight."

"What's going on?" The alarm in Micah's voice put me on edge.

"Your mom had an accident at the Citadel, fell down some stairs. She was taken to the clinic."

Micah was out of his seat in a flash. "I have to go." Micah looked between me and his friend, clearly torn.

As much as I wanted to go with him and check on Mrs. Ilsan, I needed to make the most of the opportunity, even if it was wrong to do so. "Go on first, I'll take Etienne and meet you there." I smiled reassuringly.

"No, no, stay here. I don't want you walking the streets alone. I'll come back once I get my mom settled. Just wait for me, okay?" He kissed my head and hurried into the throng with his friend.

Guilt roiled in my stomach, but I shoved it away. Mrs. Ilsan would be fine. I had other, possibly world-altering, things to worry about.

Micah had confirmed what Shroding had said about the Wraiths. Now I needed to confirm what I'd read in the yellow book.

I shimmied my way through the crowd with as much grace as a newborn kitten. I found myself wishing I'd stayed home in bed working on the farm ledgers. Bodies and hands were everywhere, making me anxious. I wrapped my coat tightly around me, feeling the yellow journal in my pocket. Determined, I unceremoniously shoved my way up the stairs, ignoring the protests around me. This would be my last clubbing experience for a while.

CHAPTER 18
Bricks & Bones

The music faded into the background as I broke from the crowd and raced up the stairs into the storefront. I slipped out onto the street. The clock tower told me the library would close in the next thirty minutes. Thankfully, it was only a five-minute walk from the club, but I didn't walk, I ran, in heels, which was almost as deadly as grappling with the Wraiths. With limited time on my hands, I didn't want to waste a second using it for a stroll.

When I arrived I found the lobby empty save for a single attendant. I did not wait for her to see me and jogged right up to her desk.

"Hello, dear, oh my, you look frazzled. Are you okay, do you need help?" She spoke with hand gestures as wild as her unkempt red hair.

"No," I breathed, "I'm fine. I was actually wondering if you have any books like this one"—I pulled the yellow journal from my pocket and laid it on the counter between us—"or if you have seen anything like it before?"

"This book..." She lifted it and seemed to marvel over the

smooth leather and burnt pages. "It has no publication information, no title. No, I don't have one like this here." She paused for a moment, her fingers brushing the gold-trimmed pages, eyes squinting. "We do have one that is yellow and trimmed in gold, but it's not a leather book."

It was a start. Even if the two books were unrelated, I needed to leave no stone unturned.

"What is the book you have?" I asked.

"It's a copy of one of the king's journals from when the Seraphs got their power. It is often used for historical studies. We only have that one book trimmed in gold. It was made to look just like the original, which I think is still at the palace in Romath."

"Could I see the copy you have here?" I asked, taking my book gently from her boisterous hands.

"Of course, dear. Anything for a fellow scholar." She winked and disappeared for a long time. She was gone so long I almost thought she had forgotten about me. I fidgeted at the counter, hoping I had enough time to get back to the club before Micah. Finally the older lady came back holding a small yellow book.

"Here we are. I'll just be over there when you're done." She walked to the far side of the counter.

I touched the book hesitantly, as if it would feel like sandpaper too. It didn't. In fact there was nothing particularly special about this book from what I could tell.

I opened it and nearly dropped it in shock. Outwardly it was not impressive, but inside, though most of the words had been typed out, some of the king's handwriting had been copied from the original. Hastily I compared the writing inside my book. There was no doubt the penmanship was the same. Even the letters written in another language were in the library's yellow book as well. But how could it be the same handwriting? That would mean that the book in my hand was one of the late king's journals. How in the world had it ended up on our farm, in our attic, under a floorboard? How had something so important, something with a prophecy that could change the world, ended up on a farm in Wycliff, and even more unbelievably in my hands?

I didn't need any further proof of the book's origin. My family was connected to the royal family, to the late King Roark and to his son; Prince Shroding. Who I was connected to somehow in my sleep, and who was connected to the strange, beautiful cat; Iri. Shroding had said he needed to be saved. He had said I had the gift—was he right about that too? I looked at my hands, trying to feel if anything was different about me.

Nothing. I didn't feel anything.

"I'm sorry, dear, but we are closing now." The red-haired lady came back, her face deeply saddened. "I hate telling people to leave, hungry minds should be allowed to explore unruled by time. Like the great Seraphs." She sighed longingly.

"It's okay, ma'am. I'm finished. Thank you for your time." I gave her a quick wave, tucking my book into my pocket. I walked back to the club, distracted. My thoughts swirled. When I got home I would find Iri and get to the bottom of things. I would force myself to sleep until I found myself in the place where Shroding was. I would figure out how I was supposed to save him.

I turned into the dead-end alley next to the club, needing some quiet to think, to brace myself before entering the throng of bodies and suffocating heat inside.

Large trash bins lined the brick wall opposite the main

road. I turned, toeing a bag that clinked, clearly full of glass bottles. At least they separated their trash. I peered up at the sky; the light pollution was just enough to hide all the stars.

"Where are you, Shroding?" I whispered to the starless night.

"What do we have here?" A male voice startled me. I turned to see the alley exit blocked by a group of men. Not regular men... soldiers from the Citadel.

"How old are you, pretty thing?" one in a gray jumpsuit asked. His suit was a uniform all trainees at the Citadel wore. It was the same as the one Theo had worn during training when he was new to the gift. The other three men wore regular clothes, but their short hair told me they too were soldiers.

"Seventeen," I answered defiantly, as if my age was something to be so proud of. They were scary but not nearly as terrifying as my nightmares. They were soldiers of Shamar —they shouldn't be cornering women in alleys like this. "Now if you would excuse me, I was just leaving." I recognized one of the boys. He looked at me and raised his eyebrows.

"You live around here? Odd that you would be seventeen and not be training for enlistment," the jumpsuit boy said.

What was he talking about? Was he just too drunk to know what he was saying?

"Your vibration is really strong. Do you have any idea how useful that would be?" another commented. It was the man with the mole on his face from earlier.

"I don't have a gift," I said incredulously.

"Sure, you do. We all can feel it coming off you. Wave after wave." He licked his lips as if he could taste it. "It's enticing. Have you ever felt power like hers?" the man with the mole said, seeming more sober than he had been inside the club.

"Not from anyone on this side of the border, if you know what I mean." The guy in the uniform sneered, his gaze raking over my exposed legs.

"I don't." I didn't. Shroding's words came to my mind then. *They know you are important, and not just because you have a strong vibration ability...* So he had been right about that too?

"Lies don't look good on that pretty face," the mole boy responded, stepping towards me.

I stepped back.

"It's true, she didn't have the gift before," the boy I now pegged as an old friend of Theo's said. He had come over once or twice when we were kids, before Micah had moved to town, but they had some kind of falling out. Looked like he had enlisted too and had fallen into a less than savory crowd. I couldn't tell if he would help me or not.

"We should have her enlist right away," another chimed in.

"Oh, wonderful. We haven't had a girl with the gift up at the Citadel in a while."

"I would love to teach you some Krav movements. How do you feel about learning some ground fighting? I know some pins that will make you squirm." Mole Guy came closer, laughing a little at his tasteless joke. I knew he was baiting me, trying to scare me. I should be scared—there were four of them, and I was alone. Even if Shroding was right and I had the gift, I didn't know the first thing about how to use it.

The fear that should have been on my face was suddenly on the soldiers'. They looked at each other, alarmed. "What is that?" one of them asked, eyes wide.

What was what? I looked around frantically, not seeing anything amiss.

"Guys, let's get out of here!" They turned and began to run from me, but their feet stopped midstep, their bodies twisting, convulsing, limbs contorting as if their joints were separated and then put back together at all the wrong angles. After a moment it seemed to stop, and their bodies returned to normal, snapping back into place. Slowly they turned to face me. Their pupils glowed with an unnatural purple ring, and Micah's words from the night before filled my mind.

Wraiths. Wraiths had possessed these men. The four soldiers were no longer drunk scoundrels cornering helpless women. They were hosts to creatures so corrupt that when they were alive they'd mutilated their bodies to gain power.

I began to tremble. I could feel the darkness closing in all around me just like in my dreams. But they were not the smoky and incorporeal beings from my dreams, they weren't invisible, and their tangibility made them more terrifying than anything I had faced in my nightmares. Those monsters were able to inhabit human bodies just like Micah had said. How was it possible? Why were they after me here, now? Had Mom known what would happen to me? Was that why she'd warned me not to leave the farm?

The men—no, Wraiths—were cornering me. Herding me like a scared animal. Malicious intent radiated off them. They weren't close enough to even touch me, but one, the mole man, lifted his hand, and I was thrown back into the piles of trash. I had never been hit by a vibration power before, and it was like no other pain I had ever experienced. It was like having a full-body charley horse while my bones rattled to the point of breaking. The bags clamored under me. The putrid smell of rotting trash and vomit from too many drinks filled my nose as I tried to catch my breath.

I scrambled to get up before I was thrown into something harder, like the brick walls of the alley. My body trembled anew in what felt like aftershocks of the attack, but the sensation was different. It started at my fingertips, a strange force in my body that moved independent of my will. I threw my hand up and shot back a pretty pathetic wave, which was not surprising since I didn't understand how to harness the strange force inside me.

The Wraiths sneered at me, their purple eyes glowing menacingly, unfazed by my attack. What was I going to do?

The mole man charged at me, moving into a stance that gave him the perfect angle to lift me from the trash and toss me violently into the wall. I tried to raise my arms to protect my head, as the rest of my body cracked against the stones. A noise, something like a scream, left my lips, but it was strangled and wet. I drooled blood onto the cobblestones. All the helplessness I had felt these last weeks turned to rage inside me. I wanted to rip them apart with my bare hands. Though I knew I would never get close enough, as they were infinitely stronger than me, I still staggered to my feet, ready to try. Ready to fight back.

The four soldiers lifted their hands. And somehow I knew this next hit would kill me. I was going to die, and this time there wouldn't be a question or doubt. I was sure, because I knew *this* was real.

"Are you insane!" Shroding's voice hollered in my mind. I flinched, my hands going over my ears uselessly. "Get down!" I didn't question it. I dropped to the cobblestones.

The silver cat dove into the alley, catching me and the four men off guard. Iri rammed into two of them, sending them flying into the brickwork, their heads bouncing as mine would have, had my arms not taken the brunt of the hit.

I couldn't register how or why Iri was there, but I was glad for his guard dog nature.

Getting up, I grabbed a bag of glass bottles and raised it over my head.

Iri growled at the two men still standing, and I took the chance to smash the one closest to me over the head. Iri launched at the other, sending him sprawling to the ground.

"Haya! Run now!" Shroding yelled, and I sprang to the mouth of the alley at a sprint.

Like a spirit sent by the Creator of Strings himself to save me, Etienne galloped down the street.

How he'd gotten free mattered little as I ran, throwing myself onto his back, ripping my dress in the process. As if sensing my distress, Etienne did not break stride until we reached the porch of the old farmhouse.

CHAPTER 19

A Letter Blurred Red

The night was crisp, the stars now visible in a cloudless sky, and for a few moments I lay frozen across Etienne's back, underneath the stillness. My thoughts were spinning.

Wraiths had hunted me in my sleep. Possessed soldiers had accosted me in the streets. Prince Shroding had been right about everything. I had the vibration gift. Shroding—or had it been Iri?—had warned me not to go with Micah. My mom had warned me not to leave the farm. What did it mean? Did she know I had the gift? Had I always had it?

My thoughts drifted back to that first night, that first dream with Theo. He had said, "This burden will pass to you." Had that been real too? Had Theo been talking about the gift? But how? The gift didn't pass from person to person; one was born with the ability to access it or not.

The moon cast a white glow over the treetops and mountains, lighting up the night. Etienne's bated breath was the only sound in the cold air. The wind had gone still—not even the dry, dead wheat swayed. The night was eerie; unnaturally quiet. The same odd foreboding came over me, as it always had in my nightmares, causing me to finally sit up.

I looked around for anything untoward, but what I really wanted to see was a large silver cat with haunting eyes and a mystery to solve.

Was Iri alive? Had he been able to escape the Wraiths? How had he known I was in danger?

I took a deep breath, the glint of metal on the road catching my eye. Two figures on horseback rode swiftly down the hill to our farm. My heart seized up, and for just a moment I was sure it was the possessed men. The Wraiths had killed Iri and found me.

As they drew closer through the gate, I did not feel the malice or darkness the Wraiths gave off, nor did I see the harrowing violet eyes.

Slowly, I climbed off Etienne, a new hope spreading through my body. I was almost buoyant with anticipation. "Dad? Theo?" I whispered, and began to walk, then jog towards the men, but I couldn't see their faces. It was only two men—if it were my family returning home, my mother would be with them.

My steps faltered and stopped. My mouth went dry.

They were soldiers, the crest of the king etched into the man's breastplate as sure as realization etched into my heart. This was the news I had been waiting for. The news I had been wishing for for weeks. Now that it was here, I wished it to be carried away on the backs of the horses it had come so swiftly on. Everything I had been hoping for was now the very thing I could not stand to receive. I stood frozen in the moment, sure I knew what was about to come.

The men spotted me, though I couldn't imagine how as

I'm not very tall, my coat and hair blending in easily with the wheat around me. They slowed their horses, and one man dismounted. The other with the king's crest lingered back.

"Are you Haya Golden?" the younger of the two asked in a clear voice. He was tall, with ginger locks twisted in tight curls atop his head. He was not in armor but still looked like a warrior ready for battle, his suit tight and black as night.

"Yes." I swallowed, my mind screaming with a million scenarios. Panic filled my face as he pulled out a letter.

"Will you receive this?" He offered the missive to me. His face was as impassive as his tone.

I could not answer, so I gave a slight nod. My hands trembled as I lifted the seal and scanned the contents, my breathing labored. The words on the letter swirled around till I could no longer read them. My body slackened, whether from lack of sleep or food, it didn't really matter. I didn't have a hope in the world to overcome this agony. I tried to look up at the man who had given me the note, but this time the man in armor was standing next to him. My ears began to ring, and gray spots filled my vision. I was going to throw up. I was going to cry. I was going to hit someone. I was going to thank them and send them off. Instead I crumpled to the cold ground as everything went black.

———

They were dead.

That was the first thing I thought when my eyes opened. I must have been carried by the men, because I sat on the porch, my back resting on the doorframe, the mesh of the screen door pressed into my cheek. The two men were kneeling in front of me. The light from the porch made it easier to see their faces. The man who had given me the letter had a boyish face that seemed to cling to baby fat. The other man was older; the moon backlit his armor, creating an ethereal glow around him even though his face was haggard, and an old scar dragged down across his ebony skin from brow to the corner of his lip. Adding to his air of mystique were his two nearly crystal-white eyes and dreaded salt and pepper hair.

"Here, drink this," the younger man said, and raised a travel canteen to my mouth. I lifted my hands to take it, but he did not let go, probably afraid I would drop it, spilling water all over myself.

"I know this has come as quite a shock," the armored man said, his voice strong and soothing. "As the letter said, the hospital was attacked. Your father and brother..." He closed his eyes, recalling whatever horrors had taken place. "It was an honor serving with them. Here." He reached into a satchel and placed three medals beside me. "That everyone may know the honorable men they were."

I couldn't even look at the medals. Instead I snatched them up and put them in my pocket, ignoring the jingle they made as I moved. I looked at the two men before me, and I wondered how long they had suffered? How many terrible things they had seen, just as my father and brother had?

"You have come far." I glanced at the horses, recalling the soldier who'd taken my mother away. "The trains are still not running?" I asked, my voice weak. The men looked a bit confused and nodded. I wondered how many trips they had made to other families. How many other ladies had fainted for them to catch? How many others did they still have to see after me and report the same loss and pain? My heart, numb to breaking for my family, broke for them. To be the bearers of such pain must be soul crushing. "Come inside and let me prepare you something to eat. Rest for a while before you move on."

The younger man seemed taken aback.

A small part, the rational part, of me thought it unwise to invite these men into my home. Especially after just having been attacked by soldiers in town and with the Wraiths out there potentially looking for me. Hunting to *kill* me. Perhaps it was the grief or a lack of self preservation or the way the older man had spoken of my family with such respect that made me comfortable with them.

"We could not possi—" the young man began.

"Thank you, miss, but we must be going," the older man answered softly.

"At least tell me your names?"

"Simon, miss, I'm not to give my full name," the younger man added, a dimple forming on his cheek. My brows knit at that.

"You're also not supposed to make it obvious either," the older man corrected. "I am Liam."

"Why can't you give your full names?"

"It is part of our military class," Simon said.

"So are those your real names or...?" I trailed off. Father had mentioned a special class of military that handled unique cases. I supposed whatever had happened to my family was a special case. To be attacked in a hospital seemed impossible, but determining what was or wasn't possible was something I believed I was no longer capable of.

"Yes, they are..." Liam trailed off. "How much do you know about the war, Miss Haya? It's odd that you should know about the trains not running to Erasmus. The ministers have been working hard to keep that a secret from the general population."

I did not feel like explaining how I knew that; I doubted eavesdropping would be a punishable offense, but I wasn't willing to find out. I shrugged. "Before you go, I have one other question. I read something odd in my history book this year. About a prince possibly born to the late king," I probed.

Liam's face was unreadable. "Myths and legends."

So they knew nothing of Shroding, then?

"Have you ever heard of Wraiths?" I directed my question to Simon, whose face flushed a light pink.

"You know a lot of things you should not," Liam responded calmly.

So they knew about the Wraiths, then. Micah had said he knew only because of the work his father did. Did these men have similar jobs to the late Mr. Ilsan?

"Who are you?" I challenged, feeling like there must be more going on than they were leading me to believe.

"Your father was an old friend. For this reason only, I will tell you." Liam settled, lifting me to my feet. "We are part of a military research team in Erasmus that studies vibration sickness. Our facility has taken over the investigation of the incident that killed your father and brother. Thus we have been assigned to deliver the news of each death to the families involved, and to inquire as to how much they know."

"Why would a military research facility take over the investigation?"

"Because everyone who died did so at the hands of the Wraiths."

I gasped. My father and brother were killed by the very creatures hunting me? What did that mean?

"When did it happen?" I demanded, needing to know if the attack was somehow connected to my nightmares.

"At night some days past. The Wraiths can only move at night. May I ask how you know about them?"

I did not want to answer them, nor did I want to learn anything else. Everything Shroding had told me, everything in my nightmares, it was all clicking together. Like pieces of a puzzle that made a grim image, one I didn't want to see. I felt the weight of the yellow journal in my pocket, the letter detailing the death of my father and brother beside it.

Etienne stood where I'd left him nibbling the dead wheat. The harvest was ruined, and the farm looked as abandoned as I was. Should I go to Erasmus, should I join my mother? Would that be safe? I had the gift, so did that mean I would not be safe anywhere?

What was I supposed to do?

A horse and wagon I did not recognize raced down the dirt road. A mop of blond hair bounced in the wind. *Micah.* I had completely forgotten about him. About his mother, about my promise to wait for him at the club. I walked past the soldiers onto the yellowing grass to meet him.

"By the Strings, Haya!" Micah dismounted, throwing his arms around me so tightly I cried out. He made muffled noises like he had a million things on his mind and didn't know what to say first. He pulled back and looked me over, turning me about. "Those men from the alley were taken to the clinic. They were talking nonsense, but one of them mentioned you and how they cornered you and couldn't remember anything after that. They said their vision turned purple and they felt cold, like death sank into their bones, and I knew, it was the Wraiths. Haya." He shook my shoulders. "I looked for you everywhere. You have no idea how insane I felt."

"Micah, calm down please," I begged, taking his hands. "I'm okay. Really." Lies, lies, lies. I was nothing, I was dust. I didn't know if okay was something I could ever be again. "Your mom, is she—" I could not hear about anyone else, any more death.

"She is fine, broken ankle, but she is okay." His eyes grew serious. "Haya, we need to talk: about the Wraiths, about the nightmares, and about..." He slipped his hand into the folds of my coat. I gasped as his fingers closed over the yellow journal. "... this." He pulled it out, and the letter the soldiers had given me fluttered to the dirt.

"Micah, I—" I reached for the letter, but his hands closed over it first. He looked up to see the two military horses tied to the porch railing, and I watched in helpless sorrow as he realized what I already knew.

"Miss Haya, is everything alright?" Simon asked, the two men joining us on the lawn. It was unclear if they'd overheard Micah's desperate explanation of the night's events.

"Who is..." Liam began, recognition sparking in his eyes before he controlled it. "I see. Since you have a friend here, we will take our leave. If you need anything, we will remain at the Citadel for one more night before moving on." He and Simon gave a quick bow before mounting their horses and disappearing into the night.

I searched Micah's face to see if he knew the older man, but his eyes were empty and unseeing, like he had not even registered the presence of the other men.

"That's it, then," Micah whispered. A sadness that should have been in my eyes was reflected in his. A sadness I couldn't fully feel. He didn't cry, so I didn't. He had been through a lot today, from taking on all of the farm's responsibilities, to setting up our date and dealing with his mom's accident. Then searching the whole town for me after realizing I had been attacked by Wraiths, only to find me and realize his surrogate father and best friend had died. That was enough to exhaust an army, let alone one man.

We stood in silence, our grim thoughts taking on a monstrous life of their own, more horrible than any Wraiths.

CHAPTER 20

Happy Birthday

We supported each other as we made our way into the house.

My brow furrowed. I had been certain I had turned off all the lights when we left for our date, a date that seemed like a lifetime ago. So why were they on?

Micah's head lifted when we walked through the door. "Oh no," he groaned, stopping to face me.

Before he could explain, the pounding of feet running from the living room had me bracing for impact.

Olivia, Tanna, Erifin, Hickory and the rest of the kids jumped and scuffled out of their hiding places, yelling, "Happy birthday, Haya!"

A smile wobbled across my face as I tried to reconcile the joy directed at me with the somberness inside. They didn't know.

Micah looked horrified. "Hey, kids, you did great, but Haya's not feeling well, so let's—"

I cut him off before he could tell them what had

happened and send the kids home. "Thank you." I pressed forward, hugging each of them. "I had no idea, you got me so good this year." Picking up Olivia, I glanced at Micah, telling him with my eyes that it was okay. Let them have this one last night, one last night of joy. We would have to tell them tomorrow. Tell them that Theo and my father were not coming back.

"What happened to your dress?" Hickory asked, his observant eyes not missing a thing. I had forgotten about the rip along the side of my dress. My hair was tangled and falling loose around my head. I was dirty and probably smelled of sweat and the trash from the alley.

"Oh." I fidgeted with the torn lace.

"Haya is terrible at riding sidesaddle, completely fell and tore her dress," Micah intervened with a laugh. "Let this be a cautionary tale for you young ladies," he finished, patting Olivia on the head.

Appeased, Tanna and the kids pulled me into the kitchen, where a small round buttercream cake sat on the counter.

"You guys made this? It looks delicious," I praised, setting Olivia down to inspect the cake. A long fingerlike indent cut across the side.

"Ignore that," Tanna said, quickly turning the cake to hide the blemish. "Erifin snitched some," she accused.

I glanced at Erifin, who was hiding behind Micah. "A talent he no doubt learned from you?" I smirked, pointing at Micah, who held up his hands in surrender.

"Can we eat it now?" Olivia whined, pulling on Tanna's skirt.

"Absolutely." I nodded, getting the plates and cutlery to serve the kids.

I went through the motions deftly, as my mother would have, the moment surreal after all that had transpired with the Wraiths, the soldiers, and the letter.

We ate, and the kids played a round of cards. Slowly they all came down from their sugar high and began to yawn sleepily.

"I can take them home," Micah said as I washed the last dish.

"Thank you for setting this up, it would have made for the end of a very nice date."

Micah took the plate and dried it. "I don't even know what to say."

"Let them stay the night; it's pretty late, and we have enough room since it's only seven of them."

He put the plate away and reached for me, pulling me close. I returned the embrace.

We stayed that way for a long time.

We put each child to bed, four between my and Theo's rooms and three in my parents'. When they were all fast asleep, Micah and I returned to the living room exhausted.

"I'll take the chaise," he offered, moving across the room.

"Okay." I sighed, lying across the cushions in my torn dress and coat. I contemplated changing, but dawn was only a few hours away; I would just sleep and fix myself up in the morning.

Silence filled the dimly lit room, but my thoughts would not let me sleep. If the possessed soldiers had made it to the clinic, did that mean Iri was alive? I needed to find him, but I had no clue where to look. I closed my eyes and willed my thoughts outward as I had done earlier that night. *Shroding, where are you? I need you. I need to talk to you.*

Micah stirred. "Are you still awake?"

I turned my head to look at him. He was sitting up, hunched over with elbows braced on his knees.

The letter and journal lay on the cushion at his feet. I touched my pocket, but only the medals remained. When had he gotten the journal from me?

"I have to tell you something."

I blinked rapidly, feeling my mind reconnect to my body as I sat up.

"My father..." Micah lifted his head, flaxen hair falling to the side as he rubbed his jaw. "He said to never tell... but I can't keep this secret anymore."

I forced myself to maintain eye contact even as my stomach dropped in dread. In his gaze I could see the beginning of another apocalypse. Another life-altering revelation.

"Haya..." He said my name like a plea, making my skin cold with fear. "I don't know how to tell you this. There's more to my family and your family than just long-time friends." He dropped his gaze. "My father was a part of the King's Court, and as you already know, those in the court are gifted with abnormally long lives. When someone with this near immortality has a family, then that gift also extends to them." He paused, rubbing his palms over his knees. "So, like my father and those in the King's Court, I too... was gifted in that way. But I'm not like that anymore, I gave it up to live a normal life. A normal... human... life." He attempted a look at me, but I dropped my gaze, my hands fisting in my lap. I couldn't understand what he was saying. "I began aging at that point," he whispered. "It was around the time I met you." He slid to his knees, crossing the room to me. One of his hands fell over mine while the other lifted my chin to meet his eyes. "Do you remember when we met?"

I could feel his desperation; a desperation I knew far too well. A holding on to something you knew was already lost.

"When we were ten?" he encouraged when I said nothing. When I remained silent, he sighed. "I tried to bring this up earlier, but—"

"It was after school," I answered. "Your dad and mine had met each other in town earlier that day." My voice was hollow.

"Yes, that's right," he affirmed sadly. "Biologically I was ten, but I was born in the year 4149. I had already lived forty-four years by the day we met."

I ripped my hand away. "4149? That's impos—" I bit my lip and closed my eyes, a heaviness pressing down on my chest.

"I lived in Romath with my mom most of my life," he said quickly. "My father was alive when the king died, and after his passing he got it in his head to come out here. My father traveled back and forth for years until I was born. Then he sent for my mother and me to live here with him. We were never to engage with your family, at least not at first. I watched from afar when Theo and you were born. I watched you grow up just as my father had done with your father and, I can only guess, the generations before him. I didn't know at the time that it was part of something bigger. I didn't know what my father was doing, why we needed to watch over you."

"You lived forty-four years before you met me? You were there when I was born..." I repeated, still trying to wrap my mind around Micah's involvement in all of this. My best friend, Micah, my one safe place, was part of this madness?

"Haya." Micah sighed, his voice tight. He smoothed my hair back into the clip I had used only hours before for our date. A date, something so stupid, so foolish, a lie. "When Theo and you were born, my mother wanted to have another child. Father had hesitated for a long time. He was very committed to his 'job,' watching over your family, but eventually he relented. My mother and I started aging normally when she decided to have Misha. It was two years before my father died. Two years till he explained the importance of your family."

"What importance?"

"Your very great-grandfather was also part of the King's Court. He knew King Roark personally. When the king died your grandfather went into hiding. My father never told me why. He only ever told me we were to keep your family safe and that your family held the key to bring a true king back to Shamar. I'm not sure my father even knew the details. I think I just assumed that your family *was* the king's bloodline. I was sure of it when Theo got the gift, but..." Micah closed his eyes, no doubt feeling the grief of Theo's death anew. "Now... he is gone, and I thought... I was nearly certain he would be able to save the kingdom, I believed... that was why he had to go fight. I believed he knew he was the king."

I shook my head. What Micah believed was so very wrong. There was a king, but it was not my brother. "We are not the king's kin."

"I am beginning to see that now." Micah rubbed his thumb along my jaw, his eyes glistening for the second time that night. I wanted to look away, wanted to hit him. Wanted to make him realize the pain he felt was nothing compared to mine. Everything I loved, trusted... had died, and I didn't know what I was supposed to do with that. How do you love something, someone, after such betrayal? I had always doubted his love, and I had been right to. I was just a responsibility, one he had taken too far.

"A-All this time," I whispered, my voice cracking. "You kept this from me."

"Haya." He leaned forward, wrapping his arms around me. "I wanted to tell you, so many tim—"

I trembled with anger. "You offered *marriage*"—I pushed out of his arms, slapping his hands away—"while there were still secrets between us. Big, huge life-altering secrets! When were you going to tell me?" Tears burned my eyes. "After I promised myself to you? After our first or second child?"

He gaped at me as if I had slapped his face and not just his hands.

"For so long, Micah—you hid this for so, so long." I stood. "Did anyone in my family know?"

He reached for my arm, pleading. "I am so sorry, it was my father's wish that your family never find out. I promised him I would protect you, guard you." He stood, pain in his chestnut eyes. "That's all... at least... it should have been all."

No. No, he did not get to play that card. He did not get to use my childish feelings against me. Whatever romantic feelings I had thought I had for him, they were not this girl's feelings. Not the girl whose world had shattered in one night. I pursed my dry lips, quieting the maelstrom inside me. "I know..." I whispered, my voice shaking. "I know what a promise to your father would mean to you. I can understand that much." And the sad truth was even in the sting of betrayal I did understand. I understood the love he had for his father, the power of a promise, and I couldn't hate him for it.

"So much is changing... and so quickly. I don't think..." I struggled to inhale through the tears. A wave of nausea had me closing my eyes. The shortness of breath and swirling vision came on swiftly, even as I tried to shake out of it.

"Haya, maybe you should lie down," Micah cautioned, hands falling on my shoulders.

I refused to pass out. Not again. Not when I needed to find Iri and Shroding.

I couldn't breathe, and the tightening pressure in my core made me hunch over in pain. Like in the alley, a foreign sensation trembled through me. As if the breath I could not get to expand my lungs was instead expanding everywhere else in my body. The vibration gift crackled in me, a force beyond my control.

I needed to get outside. I needed something to quell the torrent.

I shoved Micah but with a much greater force than I'd intended. He burst backwards, slamming into the wall beside the fireplace, his face cracking against the uneven stone facade. Disoriented, he doubled over on the chaise, blood trickling down his brow and over his eye as he clutched his head.

Panic seized in my chest as I cried out in horror at what I'd just done.

CHAPTER 21
I Am

I ran. I did not look back as the screen door snapped shut behind me.

I ran. Up the dandelion hill, and into the trees.

I just kept running. As if I could escape all of the events of the night if I just kept moving.

But my mind was a sieve, and I was falling through it. I did not know how to rationalize the power in me, the words Micah had said and the loss of my father and brother.

For over a month I had been waiting for their return. For the last few weeks I'd told myself to hope where there was none. The heartache I had now was a product of my own making. I had told myself to believe. I'd forced myself to keep the farm functioning the last few weeks, telling myself it was for them. When really it was for me. I was doing it all for myself. As a distraction. This realization was hardly surprising, but awareness did not lessen the pain. The grief. For weeks the fear of losing them had hung over me as if the fear of losing them was somehow more painful than the loss itself. Like all this time I was dying, waiting to know what happened to them, but now that I knew they were dead, I struggled to feel anything. I had forced myself to keep going as if nothing had changed. When deep down I knew everything had. I had changed. My life had changed. Theo and Father were... dead. My mother was gone, and Micah was a lie I had foolishly loved and had just recklessly hurt.

What was to become of me? My world was crumbling, and for the first time ever I wondered who I was without these people. Father, Theo, Micah... my mother. I could understand my mom not coming back, but it didn't hurt any less. When I needed her most, when we needed each other to hold on to... she wasn't here. Was there something the soldiers hadn't told me? Had she been at the hospital? What if she was hurt, and so I wouldn't worry, she'd told them not to tell me. Just like that, the feelings I had been afraid had fled me forever came viciously back; like the fangs of a ravenous animal, they tore into my chest. I struggled to breathe. The fear of the unknown, the fear of losing someone else gripped at me like the plow's metal teeth and grinding gears, shredding my heart instead of wheat.

Was I to be shredded, then? Into pieces of the girl I once was?

Who was I without the people who made me, shaped me, gave me purpose? I was not ready to find out.

As violently as the pain had come, I shoved it away. The only person who could help me now was trapped in another dimension, so naturally I didn't have a clue how to find him. But I could not keep waiting. Waiting did not stop the bad things from happening, the things I was most afraid of.

I glanced at the sky, unsure how far I'd run, and felt the familiar shift in the air. The shift that indicated the start of a new day, when the sun would paint the world a soft gold.

Could something so beautiful even still happen after so much ugliness? It seemed to me the world should be as dull and empty as I felt.

I wrapped the beige coat tighter around my body, glad that out of habit I had shoved my bare feet into my boots instead of my mom's heels. The trees whistled quietly in the moonlit night, catching the soft wind between their bare branches.

Iridescent eyes flashed in the tall oak still clinging to its summer foliage above me.

"Iri?" I called, desperate to believe the cat had survived the Wraiths. A tail twitched and vanished. It was impossible to tell if it was him or another wild animal prone to venture into high places.

"Iri?" I cupped my hands, letting my voice carry out across the dark. A chill rippled down my spine, and I pivoted, fists raised as if I could fight. Though I could recognize the gift in me, I had no clue how to call upon or wield it.

I contemplated returning to the last place I'd seen the cat, but going back to town was out of the question. I may be toeing the line of oblivion, but I did not have a death wish.

I pushed through a patch of dense trees thick with age and dead overgrowth. The crunch of leaves and sticks under my boots warned me that I was walking too far from home. From safety.

I had not brought anything with me when I left, nothing to defend myself should trouble find me. Still my feet carried me like I had a choice.

"Iri?" I called, pausing to listen. I had done this several times, following the soft rustle in the leaves, each time taking me deeper into the woods; by now I was sure I had followed seven or eight different squirrels.

I was the deepest I had ever gone in these woods.

A break in the thickset trees made my heart race as I hoped I had circled around somehow to the farm. Advancing, I took in the clearing. Tall trees almost in a perfect circle ringed the small grassy field. The grass was browned and flattened to the earth. The sky had shifted to a rich indigo, marred by fast-moving clouds and swirls of glittering stars. A cloud thinned, exposing a sliver of the pale moon. As my eyes adjusted, a strange glow drew my attention to a spot in the withered grass. A spot emitting a peculiar purple hue.

I drew closer, glancing at the moon to see it shining bright, not a cloud or haze obstructing its refracted light. Yet the clearing was not bathed in silver, but instead it was alight with a soft amethyst.

At the center of the glow sat Iri, his head turned in my direction. His once silver fur emanated the impossible purple glow. Impossible because it was beautiful and wholly unnatural. Just like him. Just as he had always been from the moment I first saw him. He was unnatural, an enigma, and I could not stop staring. He drew me to him, as if I were in a trance. The words from the king's journal burned in my mind.

The power of the king unleashed
The redemption of the world made complete
Though shadows of death are released
Call for aid and do not retreat

The moon holds the hidden crown,
An amethyst shine on silver discerns
What is needed shall be passed down
Until the prince returns

I fell to my knees in the field, a torrent of emotions ready to spill out of my mouth.

The savior of our people. The forgotten son. The hero of the story. The redemption of the world. The great prince... was a cat.

The sheer impossibility of this was something I was not in a mental state to accept. Yet I had to, because I could not deny what was before my eyes. Because I had wanted answers, and was this not the very answer I sought? I had wanted to find the prince, help him, and here he was, with me all along.

Iri... no... Shroding approached me. The fur on his back reflected like precious purple stones. Purple. The color of royalty. He was the rightful King of Shamar. My king. A king destined to save us all.

A forceful feeling of awe and wonder had me reaching out to him. I did not know a loyalty like this, to behold a king. I had been loyal to my family, to my friends, but this was unlike and yet so much more than that. It was implicit. Consuming. Absolute.

Shroding purred softly as he had always done when I was near. The purring grew louder once I touched the fur of his back. I was gentle at first, hesitant. I had pet him before when I didn't know who he actually was, but it was different now. The very attractive prince was in fact this exotic cat. The cat I had befriended. The cat I had named. The cat that had saved me from the Wraiths, just like his human counterpart had in my nightmares, in the other dimension.

The way he turned his head into my cautious fingers reminded me that I had nothing to be afraid of. This was Shroding, albeit not the real Shroding. I brushed the fur from his eyes and let my hand drift down his back as I had done many times but with a reverence I hadn't known to use before. The color of his fur was surreal. A glowing amethyst that shone between my fingertips.

A gust of wind whipped through the field, sending his fur and my hair dancing in the cold blanket of night around us. Our dark slice of quiet took on a foreboding feeling. Like ice being poured down my back. It all sank in at once. Everything. Everything Shroding had said in my dreams, everything I had said and done. My father, Theo, my mother... my whole life mixed together in this inky blue night alight with the glow of something impossible. It was overwhelming. It was apocalyptic. It would destroy me.

His ears and tail were perfectly still. Like I had seen him the first day. On the dandelion hill. He was a statue molded of elegance and consequence. Though a cat, he exuded all the majesty of royalty. In the tilt of his head, the intensity of his gaze. How could I not have seen it before? How I had been so blind?

My mind rebelled against the truth I was literally touching, twisting absently between my fingertips. I watched it glitter, tempt and taunt me into accepting. But acceptance of something so impossible, so unnerving, seemed beyond my ability. I would not endeavor to uproot all of history and my own understanding until... until I heard it... heard him confess it from his lips.

As if he already understood, his dark eyes flashed, locking with mine, daring me to ask. Daring me to believe.

"Iri, are you..." I hesitated, voice wavering, "Prince Shroding?"

His answer was immediate and clear.

"I am."

CHAPTER 22

It All Crumbled Over Night

Shroding's voice in my head was like a thunderclap shaking me down to the very foundation of what I believed possible.

"Are you alright?" Shroding whispered in my mind, a cool breeze off still water.

"How..." My face scrunched, and I knew any second I was going to disrupt that still water with a cascade of tears.

Shroding held his stance as his voice confidently declared, "Haya, I am Prince Shroding of Shamar, son of King Roark. I *am* who you met in the other dimension. Do not doubt anymore."

An impossibility proclaimed from his lips, the only truth that made any sense, even though it shouldn't.

"How?" I pleaded. One last delusional chance for none of it to be real. I was running in my mind, running away from this truth because it scared me. Because as the king, he should have been on the battlefield. He should have been on the front lines fighting for his people, not hiding in the woods as a cat. Not trapped in another dimension. If he had been where he ought, then my brother... my father... they would not have died. If he had been on the front lines, we would have won this war long ago, and there would be peace, and my family would have never come to be this... broken, dead thing, irreparable.

Confusion and shame filled my face, and though I tried, by looking away, I could not hide the rage burning in me. I was furious with him. Inconsolable for my family and what I had lost. Vexed that he'd come to me of all people, and irate because I didn't want to be full of hate. My anger was meaningless and would do nothing to bring my family back. I could not turn back time and undo this revelation.

Hot tears pooled in my eyes as it became clear he was not who I was infuriated with.

I was helpless. Helpless about my family, helpless in the war and helpless now, not knowing what to do with the information Shroding had revealed to me.

Leaves rustled in the trees around us as he slipped under my quivering arms. My tears fell over his head.

"You want to run and forget this." It wasn't a question. "You don't think this is a fight you are part of." Another nonquestion. "You blame yourself for the loss of your family." He touched his paw to my taut hand, which pressed into the dirt, rocks biting into my palm. "Blame gives you nothing but pain, it gives you nothing but bitterness and poisons the hope you could have for the future. Blame me if you must carry blame at all, but know you are not helpless." My tears dropped onto his whiskers.

His words filled me like a sunrise stretching its light into a valley, melting away the chill of the night, and though I wanted to bite back, to yell, to rage on with blame, I couldn't. His words made me weak. My feelings were twisting me up inside and making me believe I had to hate to be heard. I breathed out a frustrated and shaky breath as if all my feelings could somehow be expelled from my body this way.

"Why is it I can hear you so well now?" I mumbled miserably.

"Because you are finally listening."

Clouds passed overhead, blotting out the moonlight. The amethyst glow dissipated as if it were never there. He was once again Iri in my eyes, though I knew better now. I could not help but grab hold of him, as my furry friend, and sob.

His whiskers twitched as more tears fell on them. It was almost as if he was intentionally catching my tears on his face. Taking the gentle pat of them on his soft fur, absorbing them into himself as if he could absorb the grief itself. It was then I noticed not a single tear had fallen to the ground. He was wet all over his face and ears. Some had even fallen to his paw, which still rested atop my hand.

"I, better than maybe anyone, understand what you are feeling. I lost my father and mother a long time ago, but I remember it all too well." I pulled back to see his own eyes shimmering. He studied my face, which was no doubt a blotchy mess. Slowly he lifted his head and pushed his furry cheek against mine, wiping away the last of the wetness. "This is not your fault. You can hate me, hate your brother and father for leaving, hate your mom for choosing to go to them and leave you alone. You could hold that bitterness and unforgiveness in you. You can blame yourself to the point of vengeance. Self-sabotaging every good thing that comes to you in your life because you don't feel like you deserve it," he explained, as if he knew these things from experience.

"That's not what I want," I begged, my head throbbing from the force of my sobs.

"There's another way," he soothed, wiping my cheeks again. His fur was warm against my face.

"What is it?" My voice cracked, thick with despair.

"You had no control over what happened *to you*, but you have control of *how you* live through it. So rise up and overcome."

I took in his words, knowing them to be true but doubting my ability to act on them. Did I even want to live through this, to rebuild my life? Was I capable of rising from these ashes?

"You are a part of a story so much bigger than this moment."

A break in the clouds carried moonlight like ribbons of silver over us. Once again his fur turned to amethyst, the prism of colors dancing in the strands. The realization of what he was, who he was, hit me again. He would change the world if the prophecy he mentioned was true. If he was the one to destroy Skithian.

"Earlier tonight you saved me from the Wraiths. Why are they after me?"

"Because you don't just have a powerful vibration, you have the king's power. The only power that can bring back my human form. The only power that can make me whole again."

I looked at my hands uncertainly. "What would you have me do?" I whispered, searching for direction, purpose in his piercing dark eyes.

"Earlier tonight you warned me to get ready. Now it's your turn, because this is only the beginning; if you choose to help me, you won't be coming back."

"Haya!" Micah's voice echoed through the clearing.

I froze.

Shroding went rigid beneath my palm, head snapping toward the sound. Without a second's hesitation, he leapt into the shadows, his amazing coat turning to silver in the cover of the trees before vanishing completely from my view.

Micah sprinted into the clearing, dropping to his knees in front of me.

"What are you doing out here?" He wrapped his arms around me. "Do you know how dangerous it is for you right now?"

With Micah around me, for just a moment, I wanted to forget. I could forget because it was easy to know where I fit in his world. I could let him take me from this dream, the nightmares, and maybe I could go back to my old self from before Theo and Father had left. Everything had been so simple then. I pressed into my friend's warmth, letting the moment hold me. Letting it cover the fresh, gaping wound this night had carved into me. It would feel good for a while, safe for a moment longer, but Micah had not been honest with me, and the truth was, there was no going back. Not even Micah was the same anymore.

Shroding was so different from Micah. They are two totally opposite people, with two totally different paths in life. Both affected by chance and fate. Both molded by their worlds but molding their worlds just the same. I knew how I fit into one, while longing to fit in the other. I could go back to the farm, accept Micah for everything, or I could pack a bag and go wherever Shroding needed me.

If I was honest, I wanted to fit in Shroding's world. I had never found a world I wanted to fit into more. But his world terrified me: the Wraiths, the king's power. Looking at what having the touch of importance in my life had done to it, to my family, should be enough to stop me from going to him. I should want to walk away, and yet I wanted to be alongside him on this journey regardless of the end. Regardless of how much more it cost me. I was afraid, but like Shroding had said, I could harden myself in anger and bitterness or I could overcome it. Somehow overcoming it only seemed possible with him beside me.

"Look at me." Micah jostled me, drawing my gaze. I tried to look at him, to see him, but it was like my eyes were seeing through water; my body, the clearing, it all was a million miles away. Still I tried to focus for his sake and look at him.

I took in the small cut on his temple, shame filling me. But he was not looking back at me, his eyes instead fixed on a point behind me. I followed his gaze. The lights of the farmhouse were flickering through the swaying trees. I had circled around after all.

"Haya, something doesn't feel right."

The hair on my arms stood on end, and I felt it. The debilitating weight of a fear set deep in my bones. The same darkness that had haunted every step I took in the shadow of sleep. The same darkness from the alley closed in.

They were here.

The Wraiths.

I grabbed his hand, and we ran. Frost covered the brush, the night hitting a low that made our breath white vapors on the wind.

The closer we drew to the farmhouse, the sharper the air became, like the northern winter wind had come early to the valley, slicing through with its bone chill and erasing the light of the moon with its rolling storm clouds.

We broke through the treeline coming out on top of the dandelion hill.

"Stop!" Micah yelled, throwing his arm out across my chest, halting our descent down to the farmhouse.

I followed his gaze to the shadowed valley below.

Moving though the stalks were the figures of what should have been men. But they had not been men for a long time. Subsumed by vibration sickness, the Grieving were shells of humans, nothing more than walking corpses, corrupted by their own lust for power. Not only were the Wraiths here, invisible to my eyes, hiding in the shadows just as they had in my nightmares, but so were the humans who became them when they die. The dark terrors we fought against in the war, terrors that I used to mourn, saying, "What an awful story," because I'd believed that was all they would ever be to me; a story. But like so many things in the last few weeks, this was another tale come to life before my eyes.

"What are those things?" Micah panted, his arm still blocking me. "Wait, no... those are..."

The Grieving moaned miserably as they staggered through the wheat towards the farmhouse.

"By the Strings," I panicked, gripping his arm with both hands. "Micah, the kids." Adrenaline quickened my pulse. They were in danger because of me.

"Strings," he cursed as four Grieving blocked off the front porch, lifting their gnarled hands to attack my home.

A wave of vibration slammed into us, knocking us both to the ground, and suddenly I was falling, tumbling, rolling down the dandelion hill, air filling and sputtering out of my lungs as I smacked into the cold hard ground again and again.

When it finally stopped, I was lying at the bottom of the hill. I groaned as I sat up. My dress was muddy and stained, the rip along the side worsened, stopping just under the right side of my chest. Scrapes patterned my legs, and I pulled my coat around me, looking for Micah. What had happened?

I found him sprawled on the grassy hill a few feet from me.

I crawled over. He lay on his back, eyes closed.

Panicked, I checked his pulse and breathing. He was alive but unconscious. I patted his cheek, trying to rouse him. Awkwardly I lifted his heavy arm over my shoulders. I had to hide him from the Grieving, then I could go after the kids.

From the corner of my eye I could see the Grieving blasting vibrations at the front door. The house shuddered, glass shattering under the pressure of the vibrations. They continued to attack the structure, causing it to creek horribly, the sound foreboding and pained, like an animal being tortured.

Micah roused next to me.

"What happened?" He moaned, rolling the heel of his palm on his temple and looking at me with hazy eyes.

"We fell," I rasped over the howling. I glanced up the hill to see two more Greving, like gnarled sentinels, looking down at us. "On second thought, we were pushed."

The ground swayed as we both struggled to our feet. The smell of smoke wafted through the air.

"They started a fire?" Micah shook his head as if to clear it.

I gasped as flashes of my first nightmare burned behind my eyes.

All to ash and ruin.

"We have to get the kids out," I ordered, dragging him with me to the side door off the kitchen, my only goal to save the children.

The rooms were filling with thick black smoke, but we could not see where the fire had started.

Four kids were hunched on the floor of the living room, hands over their ears, attempting to block out the horrific sounds.

"Erifin, where are the others?" I asked, falling to my knees in front of the group.

The slight boy lifted his ash-covered head, his round cheeks smudged black. "Tanna went back"—he coughed violently—"upstairs for Hickory and Olivia," he finished, the smoke-laden air thick in our throats.

"Micah." I turned, but he was already hoisting two kids onto his back and the other latched to his front. I grabbed Erifin's hand and placed it in Micah's. "Go," I commanded.

Micah hesitated for only a second before carrying the kids out of the house through the kitchen door.

A sickening crash sounded upstairs, and I moved to stand when Shroding in cat form appeared down the hallway, an unconscious Tanna draped over his back.

CHAPTER 23

You Were My Town

There was no time to contemplate how Shroding had gotten there, I was just grateful he had.

"Haya, I'm going back for the other two."

I took Tanna in my arms. "I can help."

"Get her out first," he directed.

A grinding snap had me looking up. The ceiling began to turn black as the fire spread its claws over our heads, ready to sink its wild heat into our flesh.

Shroding slammed into my side, knocking me and Tanna out of the way of the falling debris.

I clung to the child in my arms as I toppled to the floor.

"No!" I cried as burning rubble overtook Shroding, leaving only his tail visible.

Arms lifted me up. "Where are the others?" Micah asked, bending down to check Tanna's pulse.

Tears filled my eyes as I turned my head slowly side to side, oblivious to Micah's words.

Shroding couldn't be... dead.

"No!" I breathed, as tunnel vision took over all logic. Save him. Was my only thought. I had to save him. Laying Tanna down, I rushed to him using my bare hands to lift the rubble. Shroding's tail twitched. "He's still alive, help me!" I cried, the sleeves of my coat catching fire. I screamed as the heat licked my skin.

Micah yanked me back, patting my arms wildly. "Haya, get it together, it's a cat!"

"No, no." I sobbed, tears drying before they could leave my eyes. "He's not just a cat." My voice was shrill with panic. "That is Prince Shroding! The lost prince is real. That's *him*." I gestured wildly at the rubble. "I have to save him." The words came out in a rush, but I did not care if they made sense.

Micah grabbed my arm, forcing me to look at him. I could see in his eyes he was questioning my sanity.

"*I* have the king's power," I stressed, hoping that would make more sense to him than it did to me.

He narrowed his eyes looking doubtful as he hoisted Tanna into his arms. "Then use it."

My eyes widened, and though I wanted to scream that I didn't know how, acting helpless was not how I wanted things to end. I could save him, the ability was in me somewhere, so I had to try. I clenched my fists, attempting to pull out the power as I had done only hours before in that very room.

All the rage, all the fury I had pent up over the last months of waiting, months of toil, I focused it all on the rubble pinning down the one thing that could save this world.

I refused to let it end like this.

When nothing happened I focused my mind instead on the one thing stronger than my anger: my desire to save him, to save the prince. A separating sensation filled my torso, like a stretch when first waking up, arms overhead. It yawned wider and wider till it was as if my upper body was completely detached from my lower half, and I was floating up and up. Pulsing electricity sparked in my core, jerking my body, grounding me back to the present moment. Then I felt it like warmth expanding through every limb. The gift. The king's power. I pressed my hands together imagining waves of vibration building between my hands, till they were separating of their own accord, power thrashing between my palms. I shoved the force forward. The burning debris shuddered and lifted, twisting into the air and flying across the hall, shattering against the front door.

Panting from the effort and smoky air I collapsed. "Prince Shroding," I whispered, crawling on my knees to his singed fur, comforted by his shallow breath.

His dark eyes opened as I stroked his velvety ears, coaxing him to look at me. My other hand brushed over his injured side.

"Haya." He blinked. His breathing was rough as he staggering to his feet. Relief filled me. He was battered but alive.

I turned, remembering Micah. "Olivia and Hickory are still upstairs." I coughed.

Tanna was draped across Micah's back. His expression was shell shocked.

"Both of you get outside, I'll get them," I decided.

"Haya," both men protested.

"I *can* get to them," I promised, certain only monsters would be dying tonight. Grabbing a fire poker from what was once the living room hearth, I handed it to Micah. "You will have to protect the kids from the Grieving," I wheezed, my lungs struggling from the smoke.

Micah shook his head even as he took the iron from my hand.

"They are in Theo's room," Shroding said, nodding his head to the collapsing stairs.

Without glancing back, I climbed them, the smoke on the second floor too thick to see through. I covered my nose and mouth with the burned tatters of my coat sleeve. Fire crackled, having engulfed mine and my parents' bedrooms down the hall.

"Olivia! Hickory!" I wheezed, finding my way to what was left of Theo's room. It was slanted, the floor at a near forty-five-degree angle, careening down into the room below.

I spotted Hickory's body covering Olivia's, protecting her. The two children were unconscious under Theo's desk, which was thankfully bolted to the floor, otherwise it would have been pitched towards the gaping hole that was once a window overlooking the front yard. The hall behind me had become a wall of flame; the burning hole in front of me quickly became our only means of escape. I slid along the floor, patting down the fire that caught my coat as best I could.

Once I reached them, the floor was nearly vertical with how far it had sunken. I could not tell if they were still alive as I grabbed their small bodies and wrapped them around mine. Somewhere in the background an explosion rang out, the sound of the house giving up and succumbing to the will of the fire. Theo's bed lurched, toppling down the slant and becoming a burning barricade between us and our only exit.

Rage filled me as I lay back on the floor, my foot braced against the leg of the desk, the only thing keeping me from sliding down as well.

I coughed weakly, tired and pleading. What was I to do? There was no way out, with fire at our backs and bed blocking our path.

"Prince Shroding, I can't do this. I'm so sorry."

His voice reached out to me. "Yes, you can. You saved me, moments ago. You were strong before the king's power, but you are unstoppable with it. Overcome your doubts. Fight," he urged.

I opened my eyes, my vision clouded, and I tried once more to find the king's power inside me. The warmth came more readily, the recent memory of it made what had been foreign to me as familiar as Micah's easy grin.

Like I did with the rubble, I focused on the obstacle in my way. I channeled all my fury, all my helplessness. All my fear for the two children in my arms on the bed blocking our path.

Waves of pressure built around me, but instead of throwing them outward I held the vibrations close. I did not know if my idea would work, but I was out of time to come up with any other options so with a cry I dropped from my foothold and fell.

The bed split in half before us. As if in slow motion, I watched the ripple of waving vibration burst forth around my body as I free-fell out of the second-story window to the ground below.

Soft fur brushed against my face as I came to.

I watched from the ground as Micah speared the iron poker through a Grieving's head, ripping into its porous skull and clean out the other side. It crumpled to the ground next to me. I noted three other bodies of Grieving strewn across the front yard, dead.

I sat up.

"Hurry!" Micah yelled, running to the barn. Etienne was saddled and tied to the post outside. He was neighing, kicking back from the flames, which had spread into the fields. Micah grabbed the reins and hauled Etienne away from the barn and towards the front gate, where the horse and wagon Micah had ridden on earlier were waiting.

I scooped up Olivia, as Shroding draped Hickory over his back, and hurried after Micah. The barn caught, the flames lighting it up quickly with all the dry wheat inside.

"Are they all dead?" I asked once I caught up to Micah. Were more Grieving lurking about?

"The four at the house are, if there were any others the flames probably took them."

Probably wasn't a yes, but it would have to do. I placed Olivia and Hickory in the wagon with the other kids.

"We got everyone," Micah said, relieved.

"Yes," I affirmed looking over the ashen faced children huddled together in the wagon. Unease filled me. Where were the Wraiths? Liam's words filled my mind, "the Wraiths can only move at night."

I looked at the sky. It glowed amber from the flames even as daybreak stripped away the indigo night. I watched as what was left of my home burned to the ground. The final support in my toothpick world falling with the rising dawn.

"Then let's go, we need to get them to the clinic," Micah said, patting the side of the wagon and moving to mount Etienne.

I grabbed his arm to stop him. My gaze shifted as I searched for the right words. "Find Liam and Simon at the Citadel, tell them what has happened, tell them to let my mother know I am okay," I ordered, tears burning my eyes, whether from the smoke or my own futile emotions I couldn't tell. Perhaps she would find comfort in knowing that I, at least, was not dead. "Go without me." I gave him a little shove and backed away.

His brow knit. "We have two horses, there is no reason to leave you."

I met his sweet chestnut eyes. "You're not leaving me. I'm leaving you."

"What?" It was his turn to grab me, but I was quick and avoided him. The crease between his brow deepened. "You can't leave!" His voice was desperate, and I tried not to meet his hurt gaze.

"I can't stay. I would only endanger you, them," I gestured to the kids, "the town."

Olivia coughed, her wide eyes confused. I forced myself to look away.

Micah stepped in front of me, lifting my chin. "I'm coming with you, then."

"No." I said firmly.

"Haya—"

"*They* need you now. *They* are your responsibility." I flung my hand in the direction of the wagon to stress my point. His duty to me ended here and now.

"Haya, I'm com—"

"You can't!" I screamed, causing him to step back. The pain of losing him along with everything I'd ever known hung in those two words. It was the cry of my soul being crushed. "You can't..." I repeated softer. "You have your mother and Misha to think about." I trembled. "Micah, this is so much bigger than you and me. I have to go, for my father and Theo. For every person fighting in this war. If I can help stop it, I have to go. Your dad would've wanted that, and he would've wanted you to stay with your mother and sister," I reasoned.

"I swore to my father I would protect you and Theo. I failed once, I won't again."

"Then help me," I demanded, "by letting me go," I whispered, "that's the only thing you can do for me now."

Everything was happening so fast. I should have known what was coming. I should have paid better attention. I should have done more. I was such a coward, living in my own little world thinking I could ignore the warning signs. Justification was my worst enemy, and I had let it deceive me into thinking I had some control over what was happening.

I took his hands in mine and met his wounded gaze. In that moment I knew that I would have never made him happy. That he would have never made me happy. Not in the ways we both wanted. He needed someone who could spark in him more than just lustful interest and a sense of duty. Someone who would not leave no matter the circumstance. Maybe once I could have been that girl, but with Shroding at my side I could no longer be that person for him. I had to be someone else, something else.

My only thoughts had to be for Shroding and saving him. Saving our kingdom.

"I'm sorry."

His arms wrapped around my shoulders, and my reality shook once more as I wrestled with the desire to stay in the arms of the one safe place I had left. A safe place only safe by the many years it had held that role, a role now gone. A safe place that was as much ash as my home. A safe place only safe in the memory of the girl who lived in a farmhouse surrounded by the golden wheat of her namesake. Before I could lose my nerve I pulled away.

"Go back to town, go as fast as you can. Those things won't follow after you," I said, pushing him towards Etienne.

He gripped the reins. "You take him."

"I couldn't."

"Please, take him," Micah insisted. "He knows his way home—if something goes wrong, I know he will bring you back to me."

I conceded, taking the reins, but where he had hope, I understood there was no coming back.

"It feels so wrong to let you go this way, after... everything we have been through together." He dropped his head sadly, flaxen hair falling over the cut on his brow. "I don't even know when you will be back." He let out a heavy sigh. "You better not die," he teased half-heartedly.

Shroding brushed against my leg.

"You better make sure nothing happens to her, cat," Micah warned, then faltered, "I mean, prince?" He shifted uncomfortably, and I gave a weary smile, grateful to not be the only one struggling with the oddity of Shroding's revelation.

"You have my word," Shroding replied, but only I could hear. It was too bizarre to repeat, so I simply nodded at Micah and mounted Etienne.

"Where will you go?"

I looked down at Shroding, who met my gaze, waiting for my decision. A decision I'd made long ago. Since that very first night, every choice I had made was steering me towards him, towards this moment. Towards leaving.

"I will go wherever he leads me," I vowed.

At that Shroding took off, up the dandelion hill and towards the snow capped mountains beyond.

Micah tapped my knee, the simple code "I love you," causing me to bow my head in regret.

Words felt cheap after what we had just been through, so I squeezed his shoulder, letting it convey everything I wanted to say, but couldn't. Trying to tell him not to wait for me. Telling him it wouldn't be me, not anymore.

"Haya?" Olivia hiccuped, tears streaming down her sooten face. The other kids looked at me with sorrow in their eyes.

"What about Theo and Mr. Golden?" Erifin wheezed.

"You can't l-leave..." Tanna stammered, tears rolling down her cheeks, and onto the head of Hickory who lay unconscious in her lap.

I clutched the reins. No words of reason or explanation would ever be enough to justify leaving them, and yet I could not stay. Their shattered expressions would haunt me, but at least their deaths would not be on my head. With intention I turned away, and prompted Etienne to run towards the horizon, following after Shroding.

"H-Haya!" Olivia's wail echoed through the valley.

I bit my lip determined not to look back at the smoldering rubble of my home, nor the dust of the wagon departing with the last people I loved.

It all was behind me, where it would have to stay, because deep down I knew this was only the beginning.

THE STORY WILL CONTINUE IN...
From Crystal Mountains

Shroding's POV
Starlight

I ran to the throne room. My father had called me for the first time. I was a secret, I was hidden, so naturally I was forbidden to enter the throne room, as it was often full of people seeking an audience with the king. "Learn to rule the kingdom but never be seen as a king," my father had repeated to me over and over again. So I did. I absorbed everything I could, from combat to politics, from farming to etiquette. I took in as much as I could in my twelve years because one day I would be king.

Pushing open the arched wooden doors of the solar, I padded across the marble floor, taking in the splendor before me. Shiny ebony columns rose high to the ceiling, creating arches that glittered like the stars in the night sky. They held up a glass roof, accented with bronze and gold fixtures that hung down, lighting the room and dripping with rubies, sapphires, and emeralds. The veining of the marble floor shifted under my feet like water. I turned about, watching the floor, intrigued to realize it was, indeed, water moving beneath. I walked forward, as water poured down the sides of the black columns, giving them their shine and seeping into the floor, creating the marbled veining. I reached out, touching the water on the column nearest me. It was cold.

In my wonderment I had not realized the throne room was empty. Not even the king's court lingered. Where was everyone?

"Child." A heavy voice bounced around the room, shooting off one column to the next. The water on the column next to me trembled.

I looked to the dais, and though the room was void of its normal crowds, the throne of the king was not empty. A smile broke out on my face, and I ran through the ebony arches to my father, King Roark of Shamar.

He was still young in appearance though he had lived nearly four thousand years, sustained by the Creator of Strings. He did not wear his normal double-breasted suit of red and gold etched with the king's crest, but instead a dark Krav suit made for camouflage and secret missions.

It was a reminder I was not to get too close, that our secret was not to be revealed. I stopped at the base of the stairs leading to the throne.

"You summoned me, Your Majesty?"

"It is time. We leave for Palace Moreh at dusk." His face was pale, lips thin with tension. I may not get to see my father often, but the lack of rosy cheeks and an open smile told me everything I needed to know. He had prepared me for this. It was for the sake of our kingdom, for the sake of winning the endless war with Golan, but more specifically with Skithian. An evil so malicious and vengeful, it had no physical form. A spirit of death and decay, the antithesis in every way to the Creator of Strings. The creator who gave our family power and authority to lead this land. We were entrusted to rule and protect the people.

"I will prepare." I nodded, conveying I knew what had to be done.

I had to die to save the kingdom.

"No, no." The king shook his head, dark hair like mine falling free from the gold crown atop his head. "The prophecy will be fulfilled. You will return here someday," he whispered, and at those words I stepped back. The sensation of being knocked into passed over me, and I knew he had created a wall of vibration around us, so we could talk freely.

"I don't understand?" I looked up at my father, pleading. I had been prepared to die. Skithian knew the prophecy and must have found out I had been born. I knew someday Skithian would come for me. That was why I had to be secret, to be hidden.

"Skithian wants you in exchange for ending the war and agreeing to be sealed away. I had made the deal," the king said as he descended the steps to kneel before me. "However, I had another plan."

Once he explained why we would travel to Palace Moreh and what would happen there, I understood my fate was more out of my hands than I'd ever believed it to be. I'd been made to save the world, I had accepted that, but to be trapped, unable to move forward, or be human, be me... was a fate too cruel.

"How will I become a human again?" Fear filled my wide eyes as I looked at my father.

I had hoped he would smile, comfort and assure me, but I was not a little kid anymore. I was nearly thirteen and the prince of Shamar.

My father took my clenched hands in his, folding them

tightly. He closed his eyes and breathed in and out. After a few moments of charged silence, he opened his eyes, and in them I saw the comfort I needed. "You will know, I promise you. The person with the king's power will be with you even before you know who they truly are."

My brows knit. *How can a person be with me if I don't know them?*

He patted my head. "You will return at the moment you are needed most. The creator is always with you, in every breath. It won't be easy, but you were born with a weight greater than I've ever known, and though your shoulders are still small, they are strong enough to carry it." His dark eyes sparkled with unshed tears, the memory blurring as my own tears washed away the dream.

I rolled over in the snow; my large cat frame thick with winter fur shielded me from the brunt of the cold and wet. I pushed up on all fours, scanning the cold, dark mountain for threats before letting my mind wander back to the memory. It had been a long time since I had dreamed of the king. Dreamed anything at all, actually.

The first time I woke up in this body, I was disoriented. My spirit trapped in the pocket dimension my father had made for me, and my physical form altered into a large silver cat. It took time to get used to. Seeing, feeling, living between both. The extra inputs, not to mention the way time moved differently in the spirit dimension.

In the spirit dimension everything was similar to the real world but frayed at the edges, familiar but not. I had resigned myself to this dual yet half existence long ago. I once was a prince, destined for a kingdom, for great power and importance. But that was a long time ago. Before I became trapped, lost to the world, and lost to myself.

I had nothing now. I was nothing, just an animal wandering the snowcapped mountains far to the north, alone.

I walked to the edge of a jagged cliff, the snow crunching under my paws.

It was rare that I ever let my senses or thoughts linger in the pocket dimension anymore. My existence was simpler as an animal. It was easy to forget who I was. But the dream had rattled the comfortable detachment I had gotten used to.

I was still Prince Shroding, son of King Roark, and would be savior to both kingdoms.

I long ago gave up wondering about silly things like how long would I live trapped, how to get free?

The night sky hung colorless overhead. I watched with both sets of eyes as a flash of light burst through the sky, stretching overhead like a scar. Even this anomaly wouldn't have been of note had it not glittered the most beautiful shade of purple. For over two hundred years my eyes had seen without color, my senses truly that of a cat. So when that purple scar reached across the darkness like a claw ready to rip a hole in all the walls I'd built up, I could not deny the wonder and confusion that made my heart race in my fur-covered chest.

This meant something. It *had* to mean something.

Before I could even register what the light meant, I was running, bounding past the trees, leaping over boulders. Running in my cat form had always felt like flying, but with the shimmering light overhead calling me, for the first time, it was like my spirit was soaring right along with my paws. I chased the scar till my feet were raw, bloody.

In both dimensions the purple light burned in my eyes, a challenge, a beacon. A reminder that the Creator of Strings was still with me with every gasp of breath. That my father had not abandoned me but had given me a way back. A way out of this half life, this nothingness. A way to become whole.

Hope I'd never wanted to feel again bloomed in my pounding heart. A smile tore across my face, even as tears streamed down my cheeks.

I chased the light all night, through the cold mountains till the air warmed and snow melted and the purple scar began fading. The light withered and dimmed, till it was more like moonlight on water. Soft and gentle instead of hard and streaking across the brightening sky of dawn.

I skidded to a halt atop a hill that overlooked a deep valley.

Why had the light led me to a farm? What town was this?

Doubt crept in. I had kept my distance from humans for some time now. I shouldn't even be here; it was not safe for anyone to be near me. A weapon desired by both sides, I only brought pain and destruction. Though my father had intended for this form to keep me hidden, Skithian knew I was alive, or at least that I existed. He would stop at nothing to get me.

I berated myself as I moved back into the tree line to leave. The purple light had been a fluke, a mistake. I could feel the cold shadows of the trees drawing me back to safety, to isolation, when a new sensation locked onto me. Like the claw of light had reached down from the sky into my chest and pulled my attention to the farm.

The fields were full of wheat. A white two-story farm-house with a barn and small stable sat in the valley. A long dirt road twisted through an old iron gate, traveling to what-ever town lay on the other end. I could faintly see the lights of the town with my enhanced eyes.

Taking a few uneasy steps further out onto the hill, I

looked again at the faded purple glow in the sky. The glow drifted down, wrapping around a figure. Long hair shifted as the figure knelt and collected something into a basket.

A girl?

She could not be more than sixteen or seventeen. Her frame was strong but slight. Her long hair braided heavily down her back. She wore pants and a thick sweater to stave off the morning chill. An apron wrapped tightly around her waist, accentuating her curves. I could not see her coloring, but she was pretty, at least by traditional standards.

I inched further down the hill. Would she look up and see me? She didn't, and I could not bring myself to get any closer. Instead I just watched her the entire day. Watched her tend the farm. Wipe her brow from the hard work. She hardly ate. Hardly stopped moving the whole day.

The purple light had faded hours ago, but it had brought me here for a reason. I would go to the girl. Any second. I would leave this spot on the hill and find out who she was and why I'd been brought here.

Was this finally the beginning? The beginning of my second life? Could I start again? Could I escape this nothingness? I hated that these thoughts sprang to life so easily. I wanted to reach into my fluttering chest and rip the hope right out of me, but the pull to her was too strong, unlike anything I had experienced in the last two hundred years. It meant something.

The day grew dark, and to my amazement she moved her way up the hill, almost directly to where I crouched in the tall grass, watching. I had never cared much that I couldn't see in color. I remembered well enough from my childhood what colors the world had been. Yet for the first time since being transformed, I wished I could see in color. I wished I could see her. She sat on the grass, surrounded by dandelions. I waited for her to sense me. Notice my presence the way I had noticed hers. Did she not feel this pull? She was like a magnet; I just wanted to get closer... Then I was... inching over to where she sat.

She was crying. Her shoulders rocked with a heaviness her mouth wasn't voicing. I had never seen anyone sob so silently. What had made her so distressed? I was at a loss for what to do. It had been so long since I had comforted someone.

I hesitated in my approach, tempted to turn back. My presence in her life would only make her cry more, I knew that truth well enough. I had lived it. Still, despite my better judgment, I had no choice but to go to her. Her pull, the hope in me, something akin to a string already tied its noose around me and was threatening to choke me unless I went to her.

The closer I got, the more details I could see of her. The darker spots on her face where the sun had freckled her skin. The worn boots that covered up to her knees. Then there were her hands, slender and elegant, nothing like the hands of a laborer, but most interesting of all was how they shook, phasing before my eyes. She didn't seem to notice the way her hands passed between dimensions. That she was moving between the two planes of existence I was trapped in. A plane of existence that only the king, who had put me here, could access. I knew then why the light had led me here, to this farm, to this girl.

She had the king's power. The power to bring me back. To make me Prince Shroding once more.

CASSANDRA CIELO

FROM CRYSTAL MOUNTAINS

THE NIGHT, THE POWER
BOOK 2

SNEAK PEEK

Chapter 1
Lesson One: Let There Be Fire

The sun embraced the treetops, shining ribbons of gold through the encroaching night, as if a call to hope, even if things seemed without it now.

"You're falling asleep on the horse again."

I startled slightly as Shroding's voice filled my mind.

"I wasn't asleep," I protested, though my eyes had, in fact, been closed. Though I hadn't kept a normal schedule these last few months, I had still grown up on a farm. I was timed to rise and fall with the sun, and being with Shroding was the safest I had felt in months. With my body finally at peace it seemed to be reverting to old ways.

"How do you even manage that... with all the bouncing?" Shroding mused. He gestured towards where I was atop Etienne, whose hooves clopped steadily along the dirt path.

"I wasn't asleep," I insisted with a laugh, puffs of white pluming in the air with each of my breaths.

"Then have you taken up meditation?"

"I'm just resting my eyes. All these trees and more trees are giving me eyestrain." I closed my eyes again for emphasis.

"Nature could never give someone eyestrain." He deadpanned.

"Fine, fine, you win, I'm exhausted."

Etienne slowed to a stop beneath me.

A jolt of panic zipped through my chest—I was still skittish from all that had happened on the farm. There must be some danger that had caused us to halt. I opened my eyes, my panic turning to awe as before me spread a wide view of the western snowcapped mountains and the most beautiful sunset of watercolor pinks and teal blues.

"Wow," I breathed. Golden beams clung to the rock face as if the sun wasn't ready to let go just yet. I looked down at Shroding. *I know how you feel,* I thought in agreement with the sun. I had let go of a lot to be here, and though I did not regret my choice, I had not truly been ready for it either.

"What were you saying about trees?" Shroding teased, stepping into an errant pool of golden light. His fur refracted rainbows between the silvery strands.

I gazed at him with that strange sense of allegiance and wonder I had felt in the woods only last night, when I realized who he really was. The lost prince, the one born to save the world from Skithian. I was glad I was on Etienne because if I wasn't, I probably would have threaded my fingers through his fur in amazement as I had done so inappropriately before.

Distracting myself, I looked up at the fading light of day. It had been dawn when we left the farm... left Micah and the children, and now night was falling once more. Sorrow laced through my heart as I recalled the hurt on the kids' innocent faces as I rode away. The love in Micah's eyes, a love I didn't know how to return. And despite my effort all day not thinking about them, and all that had transpired, the moment I did, bile rose in my throat. Denying the grief I was in did not make it go away.

I shivered as the silent autumn air snaked through my burned and tattered clothes, unforgiving in its chill. As unforgiving as the path my thoughts had gone down. I quickened Etienne's pace, eager to catch up to Shroding, who had moved nearly out of sight.

My stomach growled softly. It would be best to find a town or village where we could stay for the night and get supplies. It would be nice to have a coat for when the altitude brought snow down upon us, for no doubt it would soon, and the frayed remains of my mother's beige coat did very little against such an eventuality. But what towns were this deep into the mountains?

"Prince Shroding?" I called, my voice timid. "Shouldn't we be settling down for the night? Finding a town or something?"

He was quiet for a long moment. "No, I'm afraid that's not possible. It will draw unnecessary attention."

"Attention?"

"I don't think you want another experience like the one from last night, in the alley."

I stiffened, recalling the possessed men who'd attacked me outside the club. Their hollow purple eyes.

"You have no idea how..." He paused, his words a jumble as he struggled to find the right one to complete his thought. "... odd... you feel?"

I opened my eyes, which had closed to shut out the

horrible memories of that night. "How I feel? Do you mean the king's power?"

"You emanate the strongest vibration to ever exist; even a novice with the gift would be able to sense that."

I was the novice, and after everything I had been through last night on the farm, I was the antithesis of strong right now. I recalled the peculiar way Thanes, Micah's friend, had looked at me in the club. He knew I hadn't carried the gift before, so had he sensed it that night?

"I can avoid crowds," I offered. The heaviness of the day's travels weighed on me, especially at the idea of sleeping on the ground with my side exposed in my torn dress. Self-consciously I pulled my beige coat over the revealed skin. I just wanted a shower and a warm bed.

"Wraiths tend to linger in towns, looking for bodies to inhabit. You would be in even more danger than you are right now."

"But—" I yawned.

"Can you trust me on this?" he clipped testily. I wanted to tell him I was starving, but I couldn't recall the last time I'd seen him eat. I imagined he was just as hungry as I was.

"Alright," I acquiesced, eyes falling closed as we sojourned on.

Sometime later Shroding spoke again.

"Stop here."

I cracked my tired eyes open, taking in the darkened path, the moon not yet high enough to illuminate the road. My legs were sore and body aching as I stretched my arms overhead, shaking off the short nap I had taken. Etienne stopped in front of a small cavern and spring. Steam rose from the surface of the water in the frigid mountain air.

A hot spring?

"Where are we?" I asked, dismounting clumsily like a baby fawn learning to walk. My legs were all pins and needles, and I leaned on Etienne as I waited for feeling to return to them.

"At the base of Corin." The smallest of the mountains in the range that stretched from Wycliff to Tyndale. "We will rest here tonight."

Gingerly I stretched my legs, trying to keep the side of my dress closed as I rolled my tight hips and throbbing lower back. When blood finally flowed to my toes again and the pins and needles stopped, I cleared my throat, which was still raw from the smoke inhalation.

"Is it safe?" I rasped, pointing at the pool of glorious steaming water.

"Yes." He nodded, tail flicking side to side. "Let it cool a little first if you decide to drink it." His voice was gentle as if he was afraid of being too loud or forthright. As if I were some frightened creature that at the slightest provocation would get on my horse and leave. Which I had no desire to do, in fact, by the way my butt muscles spasmed, I would be just fine not riding again for weeks. "I'll go get firewood," he informed me, disappearing into the brush.

It was my first time seeing a hot spring, and despite the heaviness in my heart, my curiosity had me a little bit excited, so much so that a smile split across my chapped lips. The sheer thought of getting the smoke stench off my body and soot out of my hair had me wanting to jump in, clothes and all. As if it could wash away all the memories of last night.

I inspected my clothes, the jagged rip along my side and the once pretty white lace, which was stained beyond recognition. Despite my wanting to jump in fully dressed, my clothes would have to keep smelling like smoke, as I did not have anything to change into while they dried. It was too cold to walk around in my underwear, nor did I feel comfortable doing so in front of anyone, especially the future king. At least my hair and skin would be clean. I stripped off the ruined layers, draping them over Etienne's saddle.

A twig snapped, and I jumped as Shroding dropped a small bundle of branches on the ground by the cave opening. Grabbing the beige coat and donning it, I tried to make my body small behind Etienne. But Shroding did not look my way. I guessed he knew where I was because he didn't even glance around for me either. He pushed the sticks with his nose till they leaned against each other, making a point. Curiously he stared at the pile.

"Where are you getting those stacks of wood?" I wondered, inching out from behind Etienne.

"I came here a few days ago and set up camp. I hid some firewood behind the cave." Holding the coat tightly closed around me, I moved to the mouth of the cave, where Shroding had dropped the bundles.

"How did you know I would come?"

"I didn't know, but I hoped." He ran back and forth a few more times to bring more wood from where he had stockpiled it.

I knelt, piling the kindling in the center of the sticks. How did he intend to light it?

When he bounded over, a moss-covered branch locked in his jaw, I asked as much.

After righting the branch next to the others, he said, "The vibration gift can be used to do many things."

I tilted my head, appraising the pile. It was said the gift could be used to make fire, wind, to bend water and more, as everything in the world has a vibration, but only those with honed skill and great power are able to do such things. I supposed the king would be one of those people.

"So are you going to light it?" I marveled, shuffling back a little as if the bundles of sticks would spontaneously burst into flames.

"No, I don't have the vibration gift in this form."

"You don't?"

He chuckled. "Of course not. You have the king's power, remember?"

I frowned, understanding clicking into place. The king's power was Shroding's vibration gift. Did that mean when he became human again the power would return to him?

"If you're not lighting the fire, then..." I trailed off, my hand lifting to point up at my face.

He gestured to the stack with his paw. "Haya?" His dark eyes flashed, watching expectantly. Puffs of white rose from his nose as he panted from running around in the frigid night.

My eyes widened. "I don't even know how to use the gift!"

"You used it three times before," he offered unhelpfully.

Four times actually, but I supposed he did not know about the time with Micah.

I held out my hands, a little desperate. "Yes, and each time it was in a moment of terror and high emotion. I haven't the first clue how to use it now."

He moved so he was at my side, ears perked and tail twitching.

"Then let me show you." He pushed his head against my hands till my palms cradled his whiskers, fingers under his jaw. I folded my knees under me, making myself level with him.

His fur was soft and warm, and I rubbed my thumbs over

the bridge of his nose absently. His ever present purr grew louder when I was near.

He shifted closer, sitting in front of me, his tail tapping my knee. "There are steps to training: first, you must learn the body movements. The way to feel and flow the power through you. That is how you wield it. It is called Krav, and every movement learned taps into one's power. I can't really show you the movements in this form, but I can help you with the meditation part. Meditation is what comes after learning Krav. This is when you begin to feel the power working through your body. You can move into the vibration dimension. Most can only stay in the vibration dimension a short time, as it requires immense concentration."

Wait, another dimension? Just how many were there? "Is it like the dimension I go into when I sleep?" I asked.

"No, it's very different. The only senses there are sight and sound. You can see and hear the vibrations of the world around you, but the world itself is black except for the color each living thing gives off. Every living thing—grass, trees, bugs, people—has a distinct color and emits a distinct sound."

"I can't really imagine it."

"That's okay, you don't have to imagine it, you will see it." His tail stilled, draping over my knees. "Now, shall we practice?"

"What do I do?" I laughed nervously.

"Close your eyes first," he ordered, a chuckle in his voice as well. "Breathe easy, focus on my pulse, where my jaw and neck meet. Listen for it, feel it against your fingers."

The rhythmic thrum was hard to pinpoint against the constant rolling of his purr, but when I targeted the sensation against my hands I latched on to it.

"Imagine that pulse like a string flowing from me to you."

I did. I tried to imagine the string stretching between us, the vibration dimension around us, but nothing happened. I waited, my eyes closed, my thoughts as quiet as I could make them. After a moment I sighed. "Nothing, I'm getting nothing." It couldn't be as easy as just thinking about a thing and believing it would happen, could it?

"You're trying too hard. You can do this. Don't be afraid of the gift. Trust it."

I sat quietly for a while, expecting something to change inside me, but I still felt the same, except the cold had gotten worse, and I shivered. My thoughts wandered to the hot spring a few feet away, and I wanted to be curled up in that warmth instead of kneeling in front of a nonexistent fire.

"You are too distracted."

I jumped a little and then glared. "Well, then let me focus," I retorted.

"Take deep breaths. Listen to the quiet around you. It's when you let go of trying to control your surroundings that you will start to feel them."

I sighed. Squaring my shoulders and sitting up properly, I focused on the gentle thump of Shroding's pulse. I timed my breathing to it. In and out. Listened as the rise and fall of the breeze joined in unison. Each intake of breath and exhalation was like falling, and a completely different kind of shiver passed down my spine.

"Feel the world around you expand, in the same way that when you breathe in, your shoulders push away from each other." Shroding's voice was soft, almost far away.

Hundreds of tiny pinpricks patterned over my fingertips, in time with his pulse. A sharp but warm sensation followed and spread through my hands, which still held his jaw.

Like every other time, a mix of fear and excitement

warred inside me as the gift rippled up my arms to my chest. Warmth coursed through my body, which was too small a container for the yawning heat and trembling inside.

"Now take all of it and funnel it out of you through my pulse. Through the string between us."

Though I wanted to question it, I pushed away my doubts and tried to do what I was told. The energy inside me reminded me of the evening sun when it hit the expanse of golden wheat on the farm. How the whole valley would shine, radiating golden light. I imagined Shroding's pulse to be the sun, reabsorbing its light, and my body the wheat letting go of the light, giving way to the night, to being empty.

Shroding whimpered. And what sounded like an oil lamp being set ablaze whooshed between us. A loud crack and pop suffused the air with a burst of heat.

www.ingramcontent.com/pod-product-compliance
Lightning Source LLC
Chambersburg PA
CBHW030024200726
48283CB00012B/834